"That shouldn't have happened," Luke said flatly. "I apologize."

This was worse than the contempt he'd shown from the very first moment—to have him apologize for something that had felt so right, so wonderful. Robyn looked up and saw that he was standing over her.

"No," she agreed blankly, avoiding his eyes. "No, it shouldn't have happened."

Laura Martin lives in a small Gloucestershire village in England with her husband, two young children and a lively sheepdog! Laura has a great love of interior design and, together with her husband, has recently completed the renovation of their Victorian cottage. Her hobbies include gardening, the theater, music and reading, and she finds great pleasure and inspiration from walking daily in the beautiful countryside around her home.

Garden of Desire
Laura Martin

Harlequin Books

TORONTO • NEW YORK • LONDON
AMSTERDAM • PARIS • SYDNEY • HAMBURG
STOCKHOLM • ATHENS • TOKYO • MILAN
MADRID • WARSAW • BUDAPEST • AUCKLAND

ISBN 0-373-17332-6

GARDEN OF DESIRE

First North American Publication 1997.

CHAPTER ONE

ROBYN tipped back her head and allowed the sharp, cool tang of champagne to enter her mouth. She didn't want it, not really. It made her feel slightly sick now; the satisfying feeling of warmth and lightness she had experienced after the first few glasses had long since disappeared. At this moment, she realised, all she felt was cold and stiff and tired and more than a little queasy.

She glanced up at the blackened night sky, pin-pointed with stars so wondrous that it made her feel like crying, and wished she were home, warm and safe in bed.

Somebody—Jeff, she thought, with his arms around an attractive blonde, called and waved to her, and she automatically fixed her smile—that big, bright, beautifully painted smile, the smile everyone marvelled at—and waved her champagne bottle, held so tightly, so comfortingly, in his direction.

They had all drifted away, she realised vaguely. Was it that late? Robyn carefully turned her head and saw that she was indeed now alone.

Completely alone.

From her position, high on top of the fountain, so laughingly obtained what, an hour ago?—she could see the sudden glare of car lights sweeping across the drive, hear the muffled laughter of couples leaving for home. She would have to climb down, she supposed, some time. And that would mean getting wet again; her short black taffeta dress, still damp from the previous climb, would be ruined for sure.

Robyn heaved a sigh. Still, what did it matter? She'd enjoyed herself tonight, hadn't she? Lived for the moment. Laughed until her jaw ached, danced and kissed and sipped champagne. . . She felt the sting of treacherous tears, her enemy in these past few months, lurking, waiting to consume her, and she hastily took another mouthful from the bottle, biting her lips, slightly numb from cold and champagne, to stop the tears spilling down her cheeks and overwhelming her completely. It was a trick she'd learned long ago; if you bit hard enough all you could think of was the pain; the misery and sorrow, in that instance, faded into insignificance.

After Mark's funeral Robyn's lips had been so painful that she had hardly been able to speak or smile for days—but then that had suited her fine, still suited her, although no one guessed, except Anne perhaps.

Poor Anne. Robyn pictured her flatmate's puzzled, frequently worried face. She wished she would understand; but then how could she? Anne had never known Mark properly, hadn't understood his unorthodox behaviour, his irreverent sense of humour or the way he'd detested sad, miserable faces, pointless regret over things that could never be altered.

Robyn swallowed painfully. Would he be pleased with her? With the way she had carried on smiling, stifling the grief, putting on her brave face to the world?

She glanced up now at the night sky, her eyes searching among the infinitesimal pin-points of light, and wondered if he was out there somewhere, had approved of her bright, carefree behaviour tonight. If she knew he was near, watching her from that distant, unimaginable place, then these past months of playing her part, of continuing Mark's glorious laughter and zest for life in a sort of living memorial to his spirit—well, then it would have been all worth it.

'Are you going to stay up there all night?'

The voice, rough and harsh, came from nowhere, cutting unmercifully through the warm night air, slicing into Robyn's thoughts with its jagged, hard edge.

Robyn shivered, drawing her arms protectively around her body. He was angry, whoever he was. She closed her eyes, and leant precariously against the carved statuette that had once spouted water until Justin or one of the others had shoved something into it. She would ignore the voice, she decided; he would leave her alone in a moment. Besides, recent experience told her that to try speaking now would be fatal; her mouth had, for some reason, seized up completely.

'Did you hear what I said? Come on, get down, you silly girl. It's late; your friends have all gone home.'

The voice was close now, directly below her. Robyn knew that if she opened her eyes she would see the speaker, come face to face with the resigned irritation.

Oh, leave me alone! she thought wearily. What harm am I doing sitting here damp and drunk, clinging to this pretty fountain? She giggled suddenly and took another swig from the bottle, carelessly wiping away the champagne that trickled down the sides of her mouth with the back of her hand, in a gesture that proved to this man she wasn't the least bit impressed or intimidated by his overbearing attitude. More than that, she positively hoped it would annoy; boring, grumpy men like this one deserved to be annoyed; they had absolutely no idea how to enjoy themselves.

Not like Mark, she thought swiftly; life to him was one long round of parties and fun. . .

She heard the impatient intake of breath, the muttered curse. 'Very well. Stay where you are, then!' the man said roughly. 'It's no concern of mine if you choose to sit up there all night, half dressed, not to mention half cut. Just don't expect me to ring for an ambulance in the morning when you're discovered suffering from pneumonia and exposure!'

His voice faded into the darkness. He was leaving, thank goodness! Robyn flicked open her eyes and peered into the night. What was wrong with the man anyway? Did he have no sense of humour? Silly, crazy antics like this were all part of being young. But then, she thought acidly, he had probably never been young in his life; some people were like that. Robyn closed her eyes again and determinedly sang a few bars of the latest hit record. Her thin voice wavered in the night, sounding poignant, full of sadness despite the cheery lyrics about love and good times. She missed a note, faltered, tried again and then forgot the words. I sound awful, she thought suddenly. Why am I singing, for heaven's sake?

It really was rather quiet now—dark too, she noticed,

glancing around. The strings of coloured lights that had been haphazardly entwined through the trees and the music that had pounded and pulsated from the house had been turned off.

I am alone, Robyn thought, and shivered as the wind sighed in the trees and ruffled her auburn curls carelessly around her face. She peered down at the dark water in the basin below. Funny, it hadn't seemed very far before; now it loomed large and unexpectedly out of reach.

How had she got up here anyway? Robyn screwed up her face in exaggerated recollection and tried to remember. Several hands had hoisted her up, and she could remember being carried at shoulder height, giggling and swaying—and then? Robyn shifted her position uncomfortably on the rough, cold stone. What does it matter anyway? she thought crossly. I'm up here now. She blinked back sudden unexpected tears and twisted round uneasily. Surely not everyone had gone home? Mark's friends wouldn't really have left her here, would they?

The single chime of a church clock rang out suddenly in the darkness. One o'clock.

Robyn put the bottle to her lips again—defiantly, desperately. The champagne tasted sharp and dry and it had lost its fizz. I want to go home, a small voice wailed inside. I want to get away from this place, that angry man. I want to be warm and safe in bed.

She struggled against the unfamiliar effects of the alcohol, against the almost overwhelming tiredness, and forced her brain into action, pushing away the thought that perhaps that man had been right and Mark's old friends had left her. She had to get down. That was certain. But how to? Robyn wasn't at all sure she could manage on her own. She peered out into the moonlit garden and felt a wave of desperation sweep over her. It did look terribly empty, such a change from a few hours ago when music had filled the air and swaying bodies had danced and laughed and fooled about. I'll have to do it, she thought. I'll just have to!

The stone scraped her legs, was rough against her

hands. She heard the ripping of fabric and swore quietly; the taffeta was gone for good, her best dress too.

It was an awkward thing, the fountain, and her dress was tight. Oh, hell, this was going to be more difficult than she'd imagined. Her fingers were cold, refusing to grip the edges of the stone, and everything was turning, spinning so that it was difficult to focus and to judge how to move and what to do with her limbs.

And then the champagne bottle, still stupidly held, still half full, slipped and fell. It smashed spectacularly against the the stone rim below, splintering the air and Robyn's nerves with its crash, forcing a cry from her surprised lips that echoed eerily in the dark night. She froze, unable to move suddenly, her body as rigid as the pretty statuette she clung to. She stared down at the scattered glass shimmering in the blackened water, remembered stories of people drowning in only inches of water and acknowledged her condition with a sinking heart. How could she climb down like this? Her head was swimming, her mouth was dry, her legs were like jelly. She was too stupidly full of alcohol to negotiate the climb safely. She closed her eyes and cursed desperately under her breath.

'What the hell's going on?'

He had returned, Mr Hostile. She could see him vaguely now, white shirt gleaming in the pale moonlight. Robyn swallowed and tried to work out whether she should feel relieved or even more depressed and decided after a moment on the latter. He sounded even more angry, even more unfriendly. Robyn gripped the fountain until her knuckles whitened and spoke with a great deal of effort, concentrating on forming her words so that they didn't sound slurred. 'I dropped the bottle. It. . .it just slipped. I. . .'

'Don't waste your breath on excuses. It's perfectly clear that you're drunk.' His voice was cold and contemptuous; he couldn't have spoken with more disdain if he had tried.

'And if I am?' Robyn managed spiritedly. 'What's it got to do with you?'

'It has everything to do with me!' he barked. 'I've been hosting this party tonight. I'm Luke——'

'Aaah!' Robyn screamed as her grasp on the fountain faltered and then scrambled to regain her hold. For one awful heart-stopping second she felt as if she was going to fall, here, now, right in front of high and mighty Luke. . .Luke? Robyn screwed up her brow and tried to remember what he had said his other name was. Carter, was it? No, Crawford, that was the name of the host; she could distinctly remember Justin mentioning it before they'd arrived here; it was his wife who had invited them all—well, not all of them exactly, just Justin—'Because she likes them young,' Justin had informed them, as they'd piled into his old banger of a car. 'It does her ego good to flirt with me; it's the star of the show's privilege to indulge herself with up-and-coming actors like myself—I'm not kidding you,' he had told them, 'she's all over me when we film!' And then they had all hooted with laughter and teased him mercilessly when they'd arrived, because she hadn't been seen all evening and they knew he was deeply disappointed.

Robyn sighed, and peered into the darkness again. So this was the husband. Still standing menacingly below. Watching, waiting for her to make a move.

'I. . . I can't get down,' she moaned despondently. It was a moment of weakness, of hope.

'And what am I supposed to do about that?' the voice enquired harshly. 'Climb up and get you? Is that the idea?'

'No,' Robyn mumbled, 'I can manage.'

She heard a short, derisive laugh. 'Manage? Are you aware of the state you're in? God, you've certainly got some nerve! You and your so-called friends make spectacles of yourselves at the party, litter the garden with debris and vandalise this fountain. And then—then, you consequently climb the damned thing and are too drunk and half-witted to get down by yourself!'

Robyn desperately tightened her grip on the statue. It wasn't going to be easy, arguing with someone from her inferior position, but she'd be damned if she'd let him

speak to her like that! 'I am not half-witted,' Robyn
tried to snap.

'No? Well, that's the way it looks to me.'

'Well, I couldn't give a damn how it looks to you!'
she retorted angrily. 'Just stop giving me a hard time
and leave me alone.'

'Fine by me. Just make sure you don't go the same
way as the champagne bottle; broken limbs at two
o'clock in the morning I don't need.'

Robyn gritted her teeth and refrained from answer-
ing—she needed all her powers of concentration to stop
herself from slipping. Besides, something told her she'd
be wasting her breath. Not only was this man overbearing; he was arrogant too. Men like that always insisted
on the last word. There was silence. Was he still with
her? Robyn twisted her head with difficulty and saw the
white shirt, with legs attached presumably, going back
down the path that led through the grand herbaceous
borders towards the house.

She peered again at the water below and fought with
the nausea and the dizziness and the fear. Well, it was
now or never. That hateful man obviously had no
intention of helping. If she wanted to get home before
dawn she would just have to take the plunge. And the
fountain wasn't very high, just a baby really, as fountains
went. She would get wet, that would be all.

Robyn took a deep breath and then twisted around
determinedly, forcing herself to slide precariously
towards the edge of the stone rim. If only the stars
wouldn't spin so, and the fountain. She swallowed and
closed her eyes, edging herself forward inch by inch. A
little bit more, just a little, and surely she would be able
to hang down over the edge and drop gently into the
water below. Yes, she could do it! She would prove that
boorish man wrong, if it was the last thing she did!

She managed it. Well, almost.

But then the near triumphant feeling of satisfaction
quickly changed to one of horror, as she realised with a
cry that the co-ordination of her limbs wasn't what it
should be, and she found herself falling heavily and
clumsily into the basin of chill water below.

In that awful heart-stopping moment Robyn wished the whole damn fountain with her in it would quietly sink into the ground and disappear forever. For he was returning. She could feel the heavy male footsteps running, thundering back along the path.

She lay there, half submerged, bruised, cold, but mercifully unhurt, with her eyes shut, and waited hopefully—anything rather than come face to face with the scorn and irritation in that man's face again. He already looked upon her as little more than a juvenile delinquent; now for sure she'd get the full force of his anger.

'My God! Are you hurt?'

Robyn heard Luke's voice as if from a distance, deep and unexpectedly showing a trace of concern. Before she had time to move she felt his arms around her, scooping her bodily from the fountain as if she weighed no more than a feather. He carried her close, oblivious, it seemed, of the water that streamed from her body, and carried her to the safe, dry grass a short distance away.

Surprisingly she knew a moment's regret when he released her; the warmth of his body, the unmistakable strength of his arms, had been unexpectedly exhilarating, despite the absurdity of the situation.

I am drunk, Robyn thought; I must be. She lay still, eyes closed, aware of him, aware somehow of the masculine presence his body exuded. He was examining her head with careful hands, feeling gently for possible wounds. Oh, hell! What on earth should she do? Robyn toyed with the attractive idea of playing unconscious. If the champagne bottle had survived she'd probably be in that state anyway, and it would at least postpone the inevitable for a while; she didn't feel up to coping with the consequences of her behaviour just yet. Besides, his hands, stroking away the strands of wet hair from her face, felt surprisingly nice, firm and competent.

After a moment he spoke. 'OK. You're not hurt. You can open your eyes now,' he instructed bluntly.

His voice was hard again, uncaring. Funny, she thought; in those brief seconds after she'd fallen it had sounded so different, so full of warmth, so full of concern.

Robyn, much to her own irritation, found herself doing as ordered. The voice was like that, she realised; it demanded obedience. She flashed green eyes, glaring up at the vague outline of his face with annoyance. 'How do you know I'm not hurt?' she mumbled angrily.

He grabbed her arms then for answer and hauled her unceremoniously to her feet. 'If you were hurt,' he said coolly, 'I'd know it. Besides, you hardly fell any distance; the fountain couldn't be described as high.'

Robyn tottered on her high heels and did her best to stand up straight without swaying. It wasn't easy; the world was still busy spinning and she had nothing to hold on to. 'It felt high,' she retorted stubbornly.

'Well, it would do wouldn't it?' he snapped. 'You're drunk.'

'I am not drunk! Just a little. . .a little merry,' Robyn replied, swaying precariously now. 'I can hold my drink as well as anyone.'

'Really? So you make a habit of falling off fountains, do you?' he sneered. 'And you enjoy lying in cold water fully dressed?'

She was glad she couldn't see him properly; the face that undoubtedly matched these horribly sarcastic comments would be bound to make her feel worse than she already did. Robyn turned and began to plant her feet carefully, one slow step at a time, towards the house.

'Where do you think you're going?' He was in front of her, blocking her path. A *frisson* of fear scorched down Robyn's spine and for the first time she recognised the potential danger of her situation.

'I. . . I'm going to find my friends; they'll be waiting for me.'

'Don't count on it. Your friends, as you like to call them, left some time ago. I told you that when you were sitting on the fountain. Don't you remember?'

Robyn swallowed and felt glad that the darkness hid her expression. She'd known all along, deep down, that they had left her. She just hadn't wanted to believe it. Oh, what on earth should she do now? Stranded in a strange place with this hostile man! Her dress was torn, she was soaked to the skin and. . .and she felt afraid.

Fear swept over her so completely now, that to think straight, to answer, even if she had been completely sober, would have been an impossibility.

Robyn shivered and wrapped her arms ineffectually around her slim body. The wind was picking up, swaying the menacing black outline of the trees noticeably now, blowing across her body, chilling her wet skin. She shivered again and then again until somehow it became impossible to stop and her whole body became racked with the uncontrollable involuntary movements. She felt sick too, awfully, awfully sick. She pressed her hand to her mouth and tried to calm her working stomach.

'Come on,' Luke ordered suddenly. 'You're freezing. I suppose we'd better get you into the house.' He took her by the arm then and Robyn found herself half running, half stumbling behind. She wanted to call out, to tell him she felt ill, that she hated the way his fingers, firm and uncompromising, clasped her chilled skin; but she couldn't. He was too strong and too determined. It was all she could do to scramble behind trying to keep up with the long, impatient strides.

They entered the house at lightning speed, with Robyn only too aware of the expensive hallway, the elegant furnishings, convinced that at any moment she would disgrace herself; to vomit now, before she reached a bathroom, would be the final humiliation.

Her frozen limbs were dragged up an impressively wide staircase and then along a hallway. Robyn's eyes registered the rich blue carpet, the cream walls, and then something else registered; something else mattered more than feeling sick and cold and terrible. Where was he taking her? These doors undoubtedly concealed bedrooms. What if. . .what if he meant to. . .? Panic surged through Robyn's veins. She tried to pull away from his grasp, to hang back, but he was powerful, so powerful.

'Stop!' Her voice came out as little more than a croak, sounding hollow, afraid.

Surely he heard, surely he recognised the note of panic in her voice? But he kept on leading her, kept on dragging her.

And then to Robyn's enormous relief he opened a

door, revealing a large, luxurious bathroom, and she was propelled into it.

Nausea overwhelmed her at last. She dived for the basin and with only moments to spare was instantly and humiliatingly sick into it.

'You're putting on quite a good display for someone who can hold her drink,' she heard him say sarcastically from the doorway. 'Why don't you pass out now? That would really be the icing on the cake.'

'Go to hell!' Robyn muttered beneath her breath, as she turned on the taps and flushed the evidence of her stupidity away. 'Just leave me in peace! I feel like death.'

'You look like it too,' he replied bluntly. 'Now get into the shower and get warm,' he commanded. 'There are towels on the rail and a robe behind the door. Come down to the kitchen when you've finished and then I'll decide what to do with you. Oh, and hurry up—I would like to get some sleep tonight.'

He shut the door abruptly and Robyn glared after him. What a swine! What an absolute swine! She looked up into the gilt-edged mirror above the basin and cursed silently. Of all the people she could have been stuck with at a time like this!

Never, she promised herself. Never again would she land herself in such a mess.

It took Robyn ages to peel away the sodden material from her frigid skin. Her lifeless fingers refused to obey the simplest of commands, and it was several minutes before she felt the spray, as hot as she could bear, pounding her stiffened body back into life, tingling the nerve-ends until she felt almost human again.

She stayed in the shower as long as she dared, knowing she must get out soon but wanting to postpone the inevitable. Eventually she plucked up the courage, half afraid by now that Luke would come to find her if she was any longer, and stepped out. She dried herself, wrapped the soft, fragrant robe around her slim body and cautiously descended the staircase.

The kitchen was to the left of the hall; Robyn could hear the bang of a cupboard door, smell the distinctive aroma of fresh coffee. She hesitated, pausing uncertainly

outside the doorway, clasping her arms around her
body, clutching the robe tightly at her neck in an effort
to feel less vulnerable.

'Well, are you going to stand there all night?'

He made her jump. She stared into the angular face
and wondered if that had been his intention. She
gripped at her robe and tried to present a fair impression
of a relaxed, composed individual. She failed miserably.

'There's no need to look quite so petrified,' he
commented somewhat savagely, hardly allaying her
fears. 'I'm no mass murderer or sexual fiend! Come on;
you look as if you could do with this coffee.'

Robyn walked forward into the brightly lit, ultra-
modern kitchen as purposefully as she could manage
and took the mug of steaming coffee he held out to her
with shaking hands. It was black, she noticed, and very
strong. She hated it that way.

'Still cold?' he asked neutrally. 'Or is that fear?'

Robyn looked at him and mustered a determined
defiance. 'I'm cold, that's all.' She sat down at the table
and sipped at the dark, bitter brew self-consciously,
aware of his eyes, cool and observant, upon her.

And what eyes they were! Robyn thought. Icy blue,
the colour of a clear, frosty sky in winter, uncompromising, startling, set in a face that commanded attention.
Why on earth had she thought him old? Her first
impressions, she supposed, had been gained merely
from his hostile attitude at the fountain. Later while
being dragged through the house she had noted the dark
hair, the strongly built body, but had hardly had time to
consider the possible age and attractiveness of her irate
and unwilling host. His startling face, the pure atheli-
cism of his body, barely disguised now by the stylish cut
of his evening clothes, made everything ten times worse.
If only he had been old and fat and balding. . .

'You seem a little more sober now,' he remarked
casually, eyeing her over the rim of his cup. 'Being sick
would have speeded that up, of course, as well as your
inelegant fall from the fountain.' He took a sip of coffee.
'Tell me, do you enjoy making such a fool of yourself?'

Robyn pursed her lips and tilted her chin, eyes

flashing at the scathing tone of his voice. Oh, yes! How superior he looked standing before her. Of course she knew the eyes had already assessed, swiftly categorising her purely on this evening's evidence: a silly, empty-headed girl who didn't know any better. Indeed, there was no doubt he had labelled her thus. Disdain was apparent in every gesture, every look. 'I accidentally slipped from a fountain and was unfortunately sick into a basin,' Robyn replied coolly. 'I don't consider I've made such a fool of myself; these things happen.'

'To you, maybe,' he murmured. 'I can't say I know too many women who would have allowed themselves to get in such a state.'

'Now look here. . .' Robyn began. 'I

'And do you allow this to happen often?' he queried, cutting through her protests. 'Or have I the dubious distinction of witnessing a rare performance?'

It was pointless, wasn't it? He had judged her, dismissed her. 'Rare performance? Oh, no; I enjoy myself like that quite often,' Robyn replied lightly, forcing herself not care, to complete the picture he had obviously already formed. Defying the need to slump her head dejectedly on to her arms, to howl long and hard that every minute of this evening had been utter hell and that all she wanted now was to curl up safe and warm in her own bed. 'I like a drink and I like to have a good time! After all,' she continued, fixing her smile, forcing herself to look into those eyes that were so deep she felt she could drown in them, 'life's too short for moping about and parties are meant to be fun, aren't they?'

'Yes, I suppose so,' he replied with unmistakable boredom, 'if you enjoy that sort of thing. Except that I wouldn't class clinging wet and petrified to a fountain as a pleasurable experience, would you?' He gave a derisive sneer. 'So, you always drink like that? Fool around so desperately? And men too. You seem to like your fair share of them, of course. Every time I looked up, at the party, you were in the arms of another man. What's the matter?' he asked coldly. 'Isn't one enough for you?'

'How dare you?' Robyn retorted angrily. 'What is this? Twenty questions? Look, I appreciate the use of the bathroom, but that damn well doesn't give you the right to stand there with that superior look on your face, lecturing me as if I were a child.'

'Well, you look like a child.'

'Well, I'm not one and I'll do as I damn well please!'

'Not in this house, you won't!' he snarled. 'This evening happened to be a mixing of some particularly important buisness with just a little pleasure. I certainly didn't need a nubile young beauty cavorting among some of my best business contacts.'

'I was only dancing,' Robyn replied defiantly. 'What's wrong with that?'

Luke's lips curled into a cold smile. 'Come, come, you're being far too modest. I wouldn't call those highly inventive moves mere dancing; they bordered on an act that would have had the best strip-tease artists in the country seething with jealousy. Oh, yes! You may well blush!'

'Don't be ridiculous—I didn't take my clothes off!' Robyn retorted angrily.

He leaned back against the kitchen unit and folded his arms, his eyes skimming over her slim figure sugges- tively. 'You didn't need to,' he replied. 'Men have tremendous imaginations. Your moves, your dress and your body were all that was needed.' He waited, eyeing the flushed face with a small smile of satisfaction and then smiled silkily. 'What's the matter? Don't you remember your performance?'

'I remember everything,' Robyn lied, 'everything, and I enjoyed every moment. So if you're hoping to make me feel guilty or bad you're wasting your time!'

'Why should I want to make you feel bad?' he retorted. 'I'm simply telling you how it was just in case you've forgotten—alcohol has a rather mind-numbing effect and after all you wouldn't want to forget even the tiniest part of so wonderful an evening, would you?'

Robyn felt sick again. She slammed the coffee-mug on to the table, put her hand to her mouth and rushed out of the room, taking the stairs two at a time. Damn the champagne, her stomach, that hateful man.

She drank gallons and gallons of water in the bath-

room. She was sober now but she felt ghastly. Oh, to be
blissfully unconscious! she thought. Then at least she
wouldn't have to endure the scathing comments of Mr
Luke-perfect-Crawford down there. But she wasn't, and
she had to get herself back to normal. She had to get
home!

'Feel any better?'

Robyn turned around. He was leaning nonchalantly
against the open door, looking, she noticed disgustingly,
fresh and handsome, despite the late hour. 'A little,' she
murmured.

'You still look pretty green.'

'I'm OK. I'd like to go home now.'

'Undoubtedly.' He moved away and Robyn followed,
instantly alert. He was about to open one of the other
glossy white doors.

'Where are you going? Did you hear what I said?'
Worry made her voice sharp. She saw the look he gave
her. Clearly he didn't like the tone of her voice.

'I do want to go home,' she repeated.

'Yes, I should imagine you do,' he said evenly, eyeing
her with ill-concealed boredom. 'Well, you're a big girl;
there's a phone in the hall—call someone.'

Robyn bit her lip and then looked down at her hands.
'I. . . I can't.'

He looked puzzled. 'Why not? Surely one of your
delightful friends would be only too willing to come back
and get you. After all,' he threw at her, 'I'm sure it was a
mere oversight that they forgot you in the first place.'

Robyn ignored the sarcasm. How could she explain
to this man that she didn't even know their full names,
let alone their addresses or telephone numbers? They
were acquaintances, no more. Simply a group of Mark's
old friends, discovered in the local pub one evening,
precious to her because of their association. Mad perhaps, but it was as if a part of Mark could be preserved
while she stayed with this odd assortment of people.
Meeting them in the evening, going on somewhere,
being among the rowdy, but good-natured crowd had
been her focus in weeks blurred with grief and pain.
Joining in meant she could lose herself, forget, live for

the moment just as Mark had always done——Oh, he had been a little wild on occasions, she knew that deep down, but Mark, being Mark, things had always turned out OK in the end. . .until that last time, of course. . .

Robyn raised her head and swallowed back the lump in her throat. But how could she tell this man all that? He was the last person in the world who would understand.

So what was it she had expected? For him to serenely offer her a lift? She snatched a look at his hard, intolerant face, her eyes lingering for a moment on the impassive eyes, the firm, sure mouth. No. No, of course not! Oh, if only Anne weren't miles away staying with her family, she thought miserably; she would have come to my rescue.

'I could get a taxi,' she ventured at last.

'At almost two in the morning?' he replied briskly. 'I doubt it, and besides we're miles from anywhere. Didn't you notice how deep you were venturing into the countryside when you and your friends arrived at this party?'

She looked across at him, saw the small, careless shrug of indifference, the impatient expression. 'Well, if there's no one you can call you'd better stay the night. If you're a good girl I'll take you home myself in the morning.' He opened the door. 'Come on, follow me.'

Robyn stayed exactly where she was. So! He really did think of her as little more than a tramp. He really did expect her to follow him meekly into his bedroom.

'Well, are you coming in or not?'

Robyn struggled to find her voice. 'What. . .what did you mean about my being a good girl?'

He yawned, dragging strong fingers through his thick dark hair. She had been wrong before, she realised; he was tired. 'What?'

Robyn repeated her question with difficulty, and saw puzzlement clouding his features until incredulity and exasperation took its place.

'Look, child,' he said roughly. 'I'm not in the habit of seducing drunken teenagers; I prefer my women a little older and a damn sight more sober. Is that clear? It was merely a figure of speech; you need have no fear that I'll creep along in the early hours to take advantage of your defenceless body.'

It was said harshly and it hurt. 'That's not your room, then?' Robyn murmured.

'No, of course not. It's a guest bedroom. Look, if you risk coming over here you'll see for yourself.' He gave a shake of his head and Robyn squirmed at the disbelief on his face.

Was it so ridiculous, then? She tried to see herself through this man's eyes, to relive the last couple of hours from his point of view. Yes. Yes, of course it was. She was an irritation to him, no more. He had made that fact clear enough. A swift picture of the sort of women he would have in his bed sprang unasked into her mind. Beautiful, of course, elegant, glamorous. In fact everything that I am not, she thought swiftly, remembering the sickly pale face with its halo of tousled auburn curls, and the huge, startled green eyes that had stared back at her from the bathroom mirror only moments ago.

'W. . .where's your wife?' Robyn asked, suddenly remembering.

'My wife?' he snapped irritably. 'What are you talking about?'

'Your wife,' Robyn repeated stubbornly. 'She invited my friend; we. . .the rest of us just tagged along.'

'Gatecrashed, don't you mean?' Luke accused savagely, throwing Robyn an ill-concealed glare of disdain. 'I'm not married,' he added abruptly, as Robyn, looking even more confused and decidedly worried, opened her mouth to speak. 'Melissa is the wife of a friend. She and her husband were called away unexpectedly—her father was taken ill. I, in a moment of madness, agreed to host this party for them. Although what business it is of yours. . .!' He glared at her again, as if she were to blame for everything, and Robyn felt herself tremble beneath his icy gaze.

He gave an impatient gesture and Robyn jumped like a scared rabbit and moved to the doorway, quickly noting the airy room, in shades of peach and blue with its single, chaste bed.

'There's a lock if you're worried,' he said carelessly, and turned away, closing the door behind him, leaving Robyn to stand cold and a little afraid in the empty bedroom.

CHAPTER TWO

ROBYN opened her eyes and, cursing quickly, shut them again. She groaned and moved her head under the bedcovers so that the sunshine streaming far too cheerfully through the uncurtained window didn't blind her. It couldn't be morning already, could it? Surely she'd only been asleep for five minutes at the very most? She emerged bleary-eyed. Where was she anyway? Nothing here looked the least bit familiar. She rose slowly, awkwardly, cursing a head that felt so heavy that it threatened to fall off her shoulders, and sat up wincing.

Oh, God! The party. Robyn forced herself to think through the fog, to recall what had happened the night before. She wished she hadn't; vivid fragments of the previous evening's escapade sprang only too easily to mind. Robyn closed her eyes and let out a groan. She felt awful.

'Got a headache, have you?'

The voice, deep and resounding, came from near the door. Robyn twisted around quickly and cursed again, narrowing her eyes against the throbbing pain in her head.

Luke was sitting nonchalantly, on a chair that seemed too small for him, legs out in front, one hand cupping his chin, watching her. She remembered his hostility through the blur of last night and glared at the annoyingly attractive face. 'There's no need to sound so damned pleased about it!'

Robyn ignored the irritating lurch in her stomach as his mouth widened into a cool, but nevertheless attractive smile. 'On the contrary,' he replied. 'I find it immensely satisfying to witness proof that behaviour such as yours doesn't occur without penalty of some sort. Hangovers can be hell, but then,' he added smugly, 'I don't need to tell you that, do I?'

She saw his eyes travel her body and Robyn wondered

what kind of a mess she much look. If it was anywhere near how she felt, it would be pretty bad. 'God, I feel terrible,' Robyn groaned, holding her head.

'You look fine from this angle.'

She saw his eyes slip a fraction, registered the all too familiar male gleam in his eyes, and with a swift glance at her gaping robe knew exactly what he meant. Robyn gave a small cry of frustration and wrapped the gown close around her naked breasts, cursing the flush of embarrassment that surged upwards until she felt as if she'd burn with the intensity of it.

'How interesting,' he drawled, eyebrows raised in cool surprise. 'Vestiges of modesty. Late in the day and rather superfluous after last night's little fiasco, though, don't you think?' He got up suddenly and placed a pile of clothes on the end of the bed. 'Put these on and come down. I want to leave in half an hour.'

Robyn, doing her best to ignore the almost over-whelming feeling of pure dislike which she had for this man, glanced at the ornate carriage clock beside the bed, registered the time slowly and looked aghast. 'But it's only seven o'clock! Why the hurry?'

'That's my business,' he replied curtly. 'Now, if you want a lift, get up and get moving. Your life might consist of lazing about all day and partying all night but mine certainly doesn't—time is precious; I have more important things to do.'

Robyn stared disbelievingly as the door was closed with a businesslike click and fought with the temper she didn't even know she possessed. Who the hell did he think he was talking to? She flung back the bedclothes and released a breath of pent-up fury, shaking her head in disbelief at that man's ill-temper, at his supreme superiority. '"My time's precious",' she mimicked. What an arrogant, pompous swine!

Luke was waiting for her at the bottom of the stair-case, fifteen minutes later, looking—surprise, surprise!—extremely impatient. Robyn felt a small curl of satisfaction and proceeded to descend the staircase at an even slower pace than before, treading gingerly so as not to exacerbate the dreadful pounding in her head.

'You've taken your time.'

'No, I haven't,' she retorted, 'considering the clothes you left me were about ten sizes too large.'

She saw him flick ice-blue eyes over her slender figure and immediately felt a surge of self-consciousness. He had a knack of making her feel like that, she realised—somehow vulnerable, excessively aware of herself in relation to him. 'You're lucky you've got something. The black number you were wearing last night was still lying on the bathroom floor in a sodden heap when I found it this morning.' He paused, scanned her face, the huge green eyes and fragile bone-structure devoid of any make-up, and gave the baggy shirt and cotton trousers another look. 'It's an improvement on last night's get-up anyway. You look OK.'

Robyn ran nervous fingers through her wayward curls. She had spent most of the time upstairs trying to look more than OK, and had despised herself all the while for even trying. 'Well, I feel ridiculous,' Robyn retorted stubbornly. 'Like something out of Orphan Annie.'

'Oh, well, my apologies,' he snapped. 'Perhaps next time you'll inform me first before you gatecrash my party and throw yourself into the fountain. Then I'll do my best to get a full wardrobe of clothes for you, in just your size and colour.' He thrust a carrier bag at her. 'Here, your dress. Now, do you want some coffee or not?'

Robyn glared at him. This man really was the end. He couldn't even ask a reasonable question without making it sound like an insult! 'No, thank you,' she replied with clipped civility, even though she would have killed for a drink of water and some aspirins. 'I wouldn't want to put you to any more trouble. You're obviously a very busy man.'

Luke ignored the heavy sarcasm and gave her a cool look. 'Yes, I am. So let's get going, shall we?'

Outside it was a beautiful morning. The sun shone from a cloudless sky, birds sang and everything in the extensive, well-tended garden looked lush and green and fresh.

Robyn shaded her eyes, took a breath of the sweet-smelling air and wished, not for the first time, that she hadn't drunk quite so much last evening. If she'd stayed in a fit state then she wouldn't have found herself in this situation now. And hangovers were so damned painful. Well, she'd certainly learned one lesson from last night—she'd never drink again!

She looked up, towards the man who was striding purposefully away from her, and scuffed her expensive evening shoes moodily on the gravelled path. God! What a way to start the day! Bad enough to feel the way she did, let alone have to spend time with a man who treated her as if she'd just crawled from under a stone.

She saw him turn and look at her, lean and rangy, hands thrust impatiently into pockets. Hell, didn't those eyes ever look human? Anyone would think she had committed the worst crime in the world instead of simply having a little too much to drink and—well, behaving just a little foolishly. She tried to remember more about last evening. The gang had been their usual high-spirited selves, they had joked about a bit, had some fun. What was so wrong with that? They hadn't, had they, done anything really stupid?

'Are you going to stand there all day inspecting the ground?'

Robyn looked up and glared. God, how she hated that superior tone! 'And if I am?' she retorted. 'What are you going to do about it? I'm sick of the way you've treated me, as if I were a child who's misbehaved.'

He walked towards her then, nonchalantly, but with a determined gleam in his eyes that succeeded in halting the flow of complaint from Robyn's lips. He looked mean and menacing this morning, dressed in tough denims, with his ruffled hair, and dark, unshaven jaw-line. Robyn swallowed nervously, immediately regretting her spurt of defiance. This was not the time to antagonise him, not if she wanted to get home soon and in one piece. 'I treat you like a child because as far as I can see you are one.' His contemptuous gaze swept her from head to foot, in swift appraisal. 'How old are you? Seventeen, eighteen maybe?'

'I'm almost twenty-two, if you must know,' Robyn retorted.

Luke gave her a cold, piercing look. 'Well, that makes your behaviour even more inexcusable, then, doesn't it?' he remarked coolly. 'You're undoubtedly old enough to know better, to learn from past experience. This isn't the first time you've endured this morning-after feeling, is it? No,' he continued, when Robyn's eyes refused to meet his, 'I thought not. Being too drunk to get yourself home safely, sleeping wherever there's a bed—no matter whose it happens to be. . .'

'Now just you look here!' Robyn stormed. 'How dare you stand there and make these sweeping statements? You don't know the first thing about me! I'm not——'

'I've got it wrong, then?' he cut in. 'Last night *was* a one-off? A mistake?'

'OK, so I've got a lively social life! And last night it got me into hot water. That still doesn't give you the right to treat me like a child,' Robyn persisted.

'Well, stop arguing and start acting like an adult, then. Now come with me; I want to show you something.' He took her by the arm, in a grip that was firm and inescapable, and Robyn felt the sudden shock of awareness, as the undeniable strength of his body pressed close for a moment against her own.

She had expected him to lead her around the side of the house towards the gravelled front courtyard; instead he headed in the opposite direction, down through the wide grass path into the garden itself.

Robyn tried to pull away, to shrug Luke's hand from her arm, but he kept her imprisoned with a firm and uncompromising grip. 'Will you leave me alone?' she cried. 'Look, I've changed my mind. I don't want you to give me a lift. I can get a taxi or. . .or walk.'

'Stop bleating. There's no need to look like a petrified rabbit. I'm not going to hurt you. I just want to show you something.'

'And if I don't wish to see?'

'Oh, you'll see,' he replied grimly. 'You'll see.'

She glared at him, muttered dark threats and struggled with the desire to kick and scream like a spoiled chid. And then she saw where he was taking her and her heart sank.

The fountain.

Robyn's eyes roamed despondently over the scene. Bottles, plastic cups, plates, serviettes littered the fountain, were strewn on the grass.

'Not a pretty sight, is it?' His expression was grim as he let go of her arm. 'Hard to believe that this much litter could be caused by a few inebriated louts.' He took something from his pocket and thrust it into Robyn's hands. 'At least you have the decency to look embarrassed. I'll wait over there while you clean up.'

Robyn looked down at the black bin-liner in her hands, looked up to where he sat, registered the determined, quietly angry expression on his face and then looked at the fountain.

It was a beautiful thing. Simple, elegant, pleasing to the eye. Perfect in the circular grass clearing. She hadn't noticed it last night.

She walked towards its edge and saw the slivers of glass shining in the morning sunlight, the remains of the champagne bottle. They glared up at her, a testimony to her stupidity.

A sudden wave of despondency washed over Robyn as her gaze drifted towards the statuette and she remembered the way she had felt up there only a few hours before. She had been thinking of Mark and she had felt cold and lonely, so lonely. . .

Why? she thought now. Why did life have to be so hard? So painful? It was such a struggle, carrying on sometimes. Mark's death—but no. . .no, she mustn't think of him now, not now. Not with this hateful man waiting, watching. He had assumed, discriminated, made her feel as if she had to apologise for the way she lived her life, when he knew nothing, nothing of her circumstances or her reasons. I don't deserve his condemnation, she thought. I don't! But I will not humiliate myself by trying to justify what I do. She took a breath and struggled with the tears. She mustn't start feeling weak and full of self-pity now.

She looked at the pretty fountain again and gave a small sigh. It was a mess. Oh, hell, I'll have to apologise, she thought swiftly. This is a disgrace and by my very association I'm guilty. He really has got a right to be angry.

She turned and walked towards him. She wished she didn't feel quite so aware of him, aware of the bleached denims, tight against his thighs, of his cool cotton shirt, open at the neck, revealing dark curly hair on a chest that was tanned and golden, of the ice-blue eyes that were hostile and not about to make her task any easier.

She hesitated, struggling with the words that were difficult but that needed to be said. 'Look, I realise that I'm——'

Luke's eyes narrowed. 'Don't waste time trying to wriggle out of your responsibilities,' he interrupted coldly. 'Just get over there and start working. I haven't got all morning. This is your mess and you can damn well clear it up!'

'Damn you!' Robyn heard herself say shakily. 'Damn you! I was about to apologise!' She glared at him furiously and threw the bag on to the ground in uncaring fury. 'You can go to hell!' she yelled. 'No one speaks to me like that! You are the most ill-mannered, arrogant man it has ever been my misfortune to meet and if you think that I am going to obediently trot over there and start picking up that rubbish now. . .'

She turned, heart pounding, head spinning with the unjustness of his whole attitude, and marched back towards the house, oblivious of everything except her need to get away from that detestable man.

He caught up with her in a couple of strides. She felt his hand on her arm and tried to shrug it off, tried to keep moving. But he turned her around with one swift jerk and forced her to face him.

Robyn glared up at him, her breath coming hard and fast in her throat, as she tried to prise his fingers away. They were too strong. 'Let go!' she spat angrily. 'I'm sick of the way you've treated me. What gives you the right to speak to people the way you do? OK, so I acted a little foolishly last night; I'm not perfect, I realise that, but anyone would think that I——'

'Will you be quiet for a moment and stop struggling?' he growled.

'Let me go, then!' Robyn insisted. 'Stop bullying me!'

He hesitated. 'I will, but calm down and for heaven's sakes stand still!'

As soon as his fingers had released their hold Robyn turned and ran. Her slim legs flew along the wide grass path as if her life depended on it. She wasn't quite sure where she hoped to get to, what she hoped to achieve, but it felt right. All the tension and nervousness and anger was released in one swift exit from the man who had dominated, despised and ridiculed her ever since they had first met.

It took him slightly longer to reach her this time—four, maybe five strides. He caught her by the waist, in a half rugby tackle, lifted her up, spun her around and in one fell swoop had hoisted her on to his shoulders even before she realised what was happening.

Robyn knew humiliation then. She beat her fists on his back, kicked and shouted and threatened, all to no avail. He carried her as if she were no more than a disobedient child back down the path to the fountain.

'Now will you behave,' he murmured quietly, 'or do I have to teach you a lesson?' He lowered her over the fountain until Robyn could see her own reflection in the water. 'Well?'

Robyn instinctively shut her eyes, and gripped the folds of his shirt.

'You wouldn't dare!' she whispered.

'Wouldn't I?' he enquired silkily, lowering her dangerously near. 'Do you want to be proved wrong?'

'No!' Robyn said quickly. 'No. Put me down.'

He carried her over to the bench, kicked the dustbin-liner away and set her down gently. 'Look at me,' he instructed, tilting her chin, forcing her to meet his gaze.

Robyn felt her mouth dry, tried to ignore the sudden lurch in the pit of her stomach as his fingers scorched her skin. He held her with those ice-blue pools for what seemed an eternity, draining her resistance, mesmerising her. And then she heard the words that surprised and startled her, confused her, so that the green eyes that flashed and sparked with anger softened and melted as she looked at him and heard each gently spoken syllable.

'I'm sorry.'

Robyn swallowed and released a small breath. 'Y. . .you're sorry?' she whispered.

Luke nodded and Robyn waited for him to release her, waited for the agony and the ecstasy of his touch to end. But his fingers stayed, torturing her with their gentleness. 'Yes. It was unfair of me; I shouldn't have interrupted.'

Robyn swallowed, tried to regain some of the antagonism, but his eyes, unfathomable and hypnotic, made her tremble, made her feel time had stood still. She watched as his gaze fell to her mouth, focused on the soft red fullness, and felt the breath still within her.

Oh, he was close. Too close! She should pull away, put some distance between them. Nervousness willed her to run the tip of her pink tongue over her lips, to moisten the softness, to unknowingly entice. . .

Luke's mouth descended then and took hers and Robyn felt the surge of hidden desire increasing, expanding, until she ached with the pleasure of it. His lips were hard, fierce, they explored and probed as he held her head with both his hands, his fingers stroking through the curls distractedly, almost wildly.

This shouldn't feel right. It shouldn't feel so wonderful, Robyn thought. I'm mad. Mad to let him kiss me like this. It's wrong, wrong. . .

But she was floating, up, away, soaring on the strength of his kiss like a bird who had been caged, tethered too long, and had suddenly been given the flight of freedom. The sorrow, the loneliness, the confusion disappeared with the taste of his lips on hers, with the hunger that communicated through his kiss, so that she burned with a desire unlike anything she had ever felt before.

And then, with almost a groan, he released her and stood up and moved away. If he had wiped his mouth with his hand then, she wouldn't have been surprised. She couldn't see his expression but it didn't take a fool to realise that distaste and contempt must lurk there.

He thinks I'm a tramp, she thought, almost dispassionately, and he hates what he's done, hates the way sexual desire's lured him, tricked him. Hell, I wanted him to kiss me so much! she realised dazedly. How could I humiliate myself like this? I know how he feels about me! No one could have made his feelings any clearer. The contempt, the disdain he's shown from the very first moment. But still I wanted him to. . . Robyn swallowed, touching her lips disbelievingly with her fingers.

'That shouldn't have happened,' he said flatly. 'I apologise.'

This was worse—to have him apologise for something that had felt so right, so wonderful. She looked up and saw that he was standing over her. 'No,' she agreed blankly, avoiding his eyes, so that she wouldn't see distaste in them. 'No. It shouldn't.'

Robyn got up then and moved past him, towards the fountain, like an automaton, stooping to pick up a plate, a cup, then finding the bag, opening it, placing the things inside, repeating the action again and then again, working with a frantic determination, doing her best to ignore the thunderous ache in her head. I must get away, she thought. I must. She could feel the tears waiting, welling up inside, ready to pounce as always. I'm tired and hungover, she told herself again and again. That's why I feel so low. It has nothing to do with that man, nothing! But he kissed you, a small voice reminded her. He kissed you and it felt as if time had stood still and when he stopped you felt as if the bottom had dropped out of your world. How can you say that has nothing to do with the way you feel?

She didn't look at him, not once, not in all the time it took to complete her task. He had moved off anyway, hands thrust into his denims, head down. Regretting, she had no doubt.

At last she straightened up, rubbing at the soreness in her back, aware of her hot, dishevelled appearance, of the small rivulets of sweat that ran down the valley between her breasts. She had finished; he could have no complaint now. She gave the bag a defiant twist. 'I've finished.'

'You have?' He turned, surveying the scene as if in a daze. 'Good.'

'So I'll be going now.' Her eyes were cold, bleak.

Could he see? she wondered. Did he know how much he had hurt her? 'Don't bother about taking me home. If I could just use the phone, I'll get a taxi.'

She saw his jaw tighten. 'There's no need. I can take you. I said I would.'

'Yes, but I don't want to inconvenience you any further. I've been enough trouble.'

He didn't deny it, she noticed. 'I'm taking you,' he replied, almost harshly. 'Now give me the bag.'

Robyn held it out at arm's length, glanced at it and then cursed as she saw the blood that dripped from her fingers on to the black plastic.

'Let me see,' he said quickly.

'No. No, it's nothing, just a small cut.'

'Don't be silly, you're bleeding all over the place. It needs looking at.'

'But I can——'

'Will you stop arguing and just give me your hand?'

She held it out and the shock of his touch was like fire all over again. He turned her hand over, palm uppermost, and she couldn't help noticing how strong and tanned his fingers were in contrast to her own. 'It's quite bad. It needs a bandage. We'll go up to the house and I'll fix it.'

'There's no need.'

'Don't be silly, girl, there's every need. It will get infected without a covering—and besides,' he added, with a small smile, 'you'll bleed all over the inside of my car otherwise.'

It was difficult, later, in the kitchen, placing her hand in his, allowing him to touch her, to come close. He worked deftly, and with a gentleness that surprised her, bathed the wound with infinite care, smoothing on the antiseptic cream, aware surely, as much as Robyn, of the tension between them.

He was close. Robyn could smell the freshness of his cologne, see the way his eyes crinkled at the corners, notice for the first time the thickness of his lashes, the way his ebony hair would curl if allowed to grow long. Stop it, she told herself. Stop this now. Have you no pride? He dislikes everything about you.

'There, finished.' He straightened up and released her hand. 'I've done the best I can but the cut's in an awkward place. I suggest next time you pick up broken glass you try not to be so careless. You could have cut yourself to ribbons.'

'Careless? Stupid? Will you stop talking to me as if I'm an idiot?' Robyn snapped. 'I'm absolutely fed up with it. I worked like mad to get that cleared up out there.'

She saw the eyes flash ice-cold, felt the sting of his retort. 'So you should have. You made the mess in the first place—remember?'

'Oh, yes, I remember,' Robyn shot back. 'How could I possibly forget? All you do is remind me! You've got a fixation about it.'

'Anyone who's as irresponsible as you needs reminding,' he replied grimly.

'There you go again! Careless, stupid and now irresponsible. For goodness' sakes, isn't there just one aspect of me you don't feel compelled to criticise?'

She saw the sudden gleam in his eyes, male and provocative, and realised too late how easy she had made it for him. What on earth had made her ask a stupid question like that? She swallowed and took a step back, but the breakfast-bar, immovable and robust, halted her retreat.

Robyn watched as Luke's eyes roamed over her body, lingering deliberately on her breasts and the curve of her hips. 'Never let it be said that I'm not aware of your good points,' he drawled. 'Beautiful girls are a speciality.' He tipped his head back and casually surveyed her some more, enjoying every moment of her discomfiture, taking his time, provoking her with his gaze. 'Such luxurious hair, a face that looks as if it belongs to an angel. . .but of course,' he murmured, 'you kiss like an expert.'

Robyn wanted to strike him. Her fingers positively itched with the overwhelming desire to see his arrogant face transformed by a slap. She had never met anyone who had such ability to make anger surge and fire within. She glared across at him and fought with her burning temper. Play him at his own game, a small voice whispered. Show him nothing he can say makes any difference. Come on, pretend. Fool him. 'Well, I would do, wouldn't I?' she flashed. 'I get a lot of practice—remember?'

It worked. The provocative look disappeared. It was as if he had suddenly been made to remember just what sort of girl he was talking to.

'Time to go,' he announced abruptly, and Robyn, with a hollow, empty heart, followed him to the car.

CHAPTER THREE

LUKE drove in silence. Only Mozart playing serenely on the car's stereo masked the tension between them during the drive home.

Robyn had no wish to talk anyway. She felt lousy, drained by the swings of emotions that had been an integral part of these last—what was it, just eight hours? She gazed out of the passenger window with unseeing eyes, hardly aware of the changing scenery as it flashed by, letting the music wash over her, concentrating on the familiar piece, losing herself in its beauty.

She wanted to forget all about this man beside her, just as he seemed to have forgotten about her. She had glanced at him when directions were needed, observed his chiselled profile just for a moment, saw the unreadable expression, the tightness in his angular jaw, the closed look that told her his thoughts had moved on, were miles away from the insignificant circumstances of the foolish girl beside him.

And then they were there. And a mixture of emotions, too complex to analyse, were welling up inside Robyn, as he manoeuvred the long, sleek Jaguar into a convenient space outside the house she had directed him to. She busied herself with retrieving the carrier of wet clothes from the seat behind, desperate to end this short-lived but uniquely humiliating experience and yet finding that to end it here, like this, would be the final humiliation of all.

Why? she demanded silently. Why does it matter?

'This is it?' he enquired, glancing casually out of the car window. She turned around, groping for the door-handle, and saw he was staring up at the small terraced house with interest. 'You live here?' he asked.

'Yes.'

'Above the office?' She saw him read the simple stylish

lettering that proclaimed the occupant below. 'Isn't that inconvenient?'

What do you care? Robyn thought as she glanced out of the window, re-reading the sign that gave her enormous satisfaction every time she had occasion to see it. 'No, it's not, actually,' she replied after a moment, and then added, with a spurt of defiance, in a swiftly acknowledged pathetic last-ditch attempt to salvage some pride, 'You see, the office is mine.'

'You mean you work there.'

'No,' she replied slowly. 'The business is my own. Built from scratch, out of nothing.'

He read aloud, '"Robyn Drew, Landscape Design". You?' There was no mistaking the surprise which crossed his face or the incredulity in his voice. Robyn saw it and felt pleasure uncurl deep inside her.

'Yes, hard to believe, isn't it,' she replied icily, with an expression that at last revealed some of her animosity, 'for someone so incredibly juvenile?' She jerked open the car door and got out. She felt like crying again. Why did he always make her want to cry?

'Robyn!'

It was the first time he had spoken her name and it sounded good. Magnetic. She almost turned to hear what he had to say then, almost. But then what was the use? Nothing he could say now would make the slightest difference. He had no part in her life. The heavy feeling of emptiness she felt would not be helped by listening to a man who had turned her life upside-down with his arrogance and insensitivity. So she ignored the insistent call, busied herself with finding the key to the door. And then, just when she felt compelled to look once more into the strong, handsome face, the moment was gone and the Jaguar purred into life and she heard the angry rev of the engine as he thrust the car into gear and roared away.

Upstairs the flat was empty; Anne evidently hadn't returned from her monthly visit to her parents' home in Oxfordshire.

Robyn breathed a weary sigh of relief, and threw the

carrier of wet clothes on to the floor. She needed space and time to think, time to sort out this mess of mixed emotions.

She stared out of the upstairs living-room window, at the place where his Jaguar had been only a few moments before. Why has he upset me so? she asked herself. Why?

She made herself some tea, hunted for headache tablets and slumped down into a chair. It wasn't until later, when Robyn heard Anne's key in the lock, that she realised just how long she had been staring into space, miserably going over and over the disastrous weekend, in a futile attempt to try and put it all back into some sort of perspective. She knew she was being ridiculous, but so much had happened back there in that elegant house, so many unexplained emotions had swung through her mind in such a short space of time, and she felt so wound up, so confused by it all. All these months of coming to terms with Mark's death, of setting her own life back on its tracks, even if it was only in a superficial way, and somehow, just when Robyn had thought she had it all under control, had regained her equilibrium, this arrogant man had appeared and set her world in turmoil with his derision and scorn.

Robyn shook her head in disbelief. It was pathetic! How could she be so. . .so feeble?

The bang of the downstairs door reminded Robyn of Anne's imminent appearance. She lifted her head from her arms and dragged her mind back from Luke's kiss, his taste. . .

Anne! She jumped up and saw with dismay her reflection in the mirror over the fireplace. Her clothes! Or rather his clothes. What on earth would she think if she saw her in this ridiculous get-up?

Robyn made a dash for the bedroom. There was no way she wanted to start giving explanations now.

'Hi!' Anne caught her at the door to the bedroom. She dumped her overnight bag on to the floor and smiled at Robyn. 'What's the matter? You look guilty.'

Robyn turned, threw her friend a welcoming smile and replied innocently, 'Do I? How was your weekend?'

'Oh, fine. Mum and Dad argued again, but then what's new? I saw James and Shirley and my latest nephew.' Anne followed Robyn into her bedroom, and sat on the bed. 'He's absolutely adorable, all pink and wrinkly.' She paused. 'Robyn, why are you wearing those clothes? Do you know how silly you look?'

'Yes,' Robyn replied, 'I do.'

'So?' Anne raised her eyebrows questioningly.

'I'm just about to take them off.'

'I should hope so. But that still doesn't tell me why you're wearing them in the first place, does it?' she grinned. 'Don't tell me I've found out your secret vice—dressing up in men's clothing. Very kinky!'

'Don't be an idiot,' Robyn mumbled as she stripped off the thick cotton shirt, praying for a diversion of some sort. Unfortunately her bandaged hand provided it.

'What have you done to your hand?' Anne asked swiftly. 'There's blood coming through the bandage.'

Robyn glanced down. Damn it, so there was. 'It's nothing, just a little cut, that's all.'

Anne sighed. Robyn knew that sound; it meant the game was up. 'OK, Robyn, what's been going on? I've been gone just two days, and when I return you're in a stranger's clothes with a bandaged hand, and an odd expression on your face.' She grinned. 'Now tell me, for heaven's sake, or I'll start imagining all sorts!'

Robyn turned away and concentrated on finding clean underclothes. 'Please don't fuss, Anne, I'm perfectly capable of looking after myself.'

'Have I said you're not?' Anne queried mildly. 'I'm just intrigued as to why you should be dressed in clothes that are miles too big at——' she glanced at her watch '—at ten o'clock in the morning. Whose are they?' she grinned. 'Is he someone I know?'

Robyn sighed; she knew from past experience that Anne wouldn't give up easily. 'Look,' she said, 'if you must know I went to a party, got a bit wet, borrowed some clothes and came home. Simple as that. OK?'

'I see,' Anne said triumphantly, obviously pleased with herself for eliciting this bit of information. 'So you stayed the night! Who is he? Do I know him?'

Robyn flushed red. Anne, she thought irritably, could be remarkably blunt on occasions. 'Yes, I did stay the night, but don't start getting the wrong idea. I just got a bit tipsy, that's all, and had to sleep in a spare bedroom at the house.'

'And you cut your hand along the way?' Anne enquired.

'Yes.'

'And you got wet?'

'Yes.'

Anne sighed. 'And is that it? Is that all the information I'm going to get from you?'

Robyn pulled a vivid emerald tracksuit from her wardrobe. 'Yes.'

'So,' Anne persisted, following Robyn through to the bathroom, 'you're not going to tell me who was at this party, or whether you had a good time, or even how you got wet?'

'No.' Robyn turned on the shower, casting a pleading eye in Anne's direction. 'Please, no more interrogation? You're beginning to sound like a mother hen; I half expect you to cluck at any minute.'

Anne chuckled and looked only a little abashed. 'Sorry, but you know I can't help worrying about you.'

'Just plain nosy, more like!' Robyn retorted.

Anne's eyes sparkled. 'Well, that as well. Oh, come on, Robyn, put me out of my misery. You met someone, didn't you? Someone special. I can tell.'

'Don't be stupid!' Robyn snapped. 'You're seeing things. How can you say a ridiculous thing like that?'

Anne stepped back as if she had been struck. Robyn saw her face and felt guilty immediately. What was wrong with her? She hardly ever lost her temper, least of all with Anne. 'Oh, I'm sorry, I didn't meant to bite your head off. I'm tired, that's all.' She glanced at her friend and managed a smile. 'And don't you go reading anything into that either! The party ended late and I was up early this morning.' She cast a worried glance in Anne's direction. 'I truly didn't mean to be so horrible. Am I forgiven?'

Anne patted her hand. 'Yes, of course. I am a Nosy

Parker. And I do need telling every now and then, although perhaps not quite so vehemently.'

She paused and Robyn steeled herself. She knew what was to come; she had seen that look in her friend's eyes too many times these past few months.

'But Robyn, please understand, it's not easy for me. I care about you. Since Mark's death. . .' Anne paused hesitantly. 'Well, since then, you've led such a different, almost wild life: parties, nightclubs, hanging around with Mark's weird friends. It's not like you and I worry. I suppose you've got your reasons.' She waited a moment and, when Robyn didn't reply, added quietly, 'You'd tell me if something was wrong, wouldn't you? I mean if you felt really unwell or. . . Her voice trailed away and she looked worriedly into Robyn's face. The unfinished sentence hung warily between them.

What word would she use, Robyn wondered, if she was forced to complete the question? Desperate? Unstable? Suicidal? She ran a shaking hand through her soft curls and forced a smile, even though her face felt as if it would crack with the effort. She had the sudden awful desire to yell at Anne, to deny everything she was trying to say; but how could she, when in truth she had felt at times every one of those things?

Robyn took a deep breath and forced herself to speak reasonably, calmly. 'Please don't worry, Anne. I'm fine, honestly. I'm coping. I'm getting there. After all, have you seen me moping around the place recently, getting depressed, crying? Well, have you?' she persisted.

'No,' Anne admitted, 'but sometimes. . .sometimes I wonder if you shouldn't do all those things—cry more, let it all out. I know you loved Mark so; he was your only family. It can't be good for you surely, to——?'

'Enough!' Robyn turned away, felt the sting of tears. This was too much now—on top of everything else. 'No more, Anne, please! Just leave it, OK? I appreciate your concern but this is my life, I have to work things out my own way.'

'Yes, yes, I know. I'm sorry; I didn't mean. . .' Anne's hurt expression spoke volumes.

Damn! Robyn thought, running a hand across her

eyes for a moment. I've hurt her now. And she was only
trying to help. She struggled with the desire to howl like
a baby. She held out her arms and gave Anne a quick,
fierce hug. 'Thanks for caring,' she murmured incoherently into her friend's shoulder, 'but I'll be all right. I
will. I promise.'

Robyn determinedly altered her lifestyle over the next
few weeks and Anne's face took on a less worried
appearance. She didn't go out in the evenings at all,
feeling, in truth, no desire to see Mark's old friends after
her last disastrous escapade. They had let her down,
leaving her alone like that. But of course they had been
drunk too, worse, most of them far worse than herself—
perhaps they had forgotten she was ever with them. It
was still no consolation.

The party had become a turning-point in many ways;
now, weeks later, she could look at it with a certain
amount of dispassion, view her life over the past few
months with a critical eye. Perhaps this was the beginning, a new era, a real coming to terms with the painful
knowledge that Mark would never be around again.
Robyn knew now that these last few months, the pretence, the false serenity, had done her little good. The
grief and the pain were still there, locked deep down
inside. They hadn't disappeared simply because she had
chosen not to reveal them to the world.

So her waking hours took on a new format. Now
Robyn threw herself into her work, staying up late into
the night, as she had done in the early days of setting up
her business, working with feverish persistence to complete a design. Sleep, wake, eat, work. Eat again, work,
work. . . And in less than no time the weeks passed and
the memories of that dreaded party were only a vaguely
uneasy thought in the sealed-off recesses of Robyn's
mind.

Robyn stretched her arms high above her head, releasing
some of the tension in her aching shoulders from being
hunched over her drawing-board for so long. Friday
night, and tomorrow held the prospect of a trip to the

Cotswolds to see a prospective client. It would be good to get out and about, to conquer new territory, she thought. The plans had arrived yesterday, promising enormous scope and opportunities. Robyn looked forward to a change from the suburban backyards and business parks she had created of late. This barn conversion had about two acres of totally untouched field surrounding it. The plan showed a small wood, plenty of mature trees and even a stream running along the edge of the property. It was a garden designer's, not to mention a house owner's dream.

Robyn stretched again and began to put her equipment away. She reached for the desk lamp and was just about to turn off the light when the sudden glare of car headlights flashed into the office, illuminating everything. She frowned and glanced at her watch. It was late, past midnight.

She hesitated a second and then as the headlights dimmed she went across to the window and peered through the Venetian blind.

It took a moment to convince herself that the tall, dark, imposing figure leaving the long, opulent vehicle really was Luke. Robyn let the blind drop with a clatter and waited motionless, while a mixture of emotions—panic among them—churned around inside her stomach. What was he doing here, now, at this hour of the night? What in the world could he possibly want?

Robyn glanced down dejectedly at her scruffy jeans and paint-splattered top and then waited five seconds after the short, insistent ring, before peering suspiciously around the door.

He looked incredible. Dressed in a dark, immaculate evening suit and a crisp white shirt, worn with a bow-tie that had been, by the looks of it, impatiently pulled apart at the very earliest opportunity. Robyn noticed every detail in a fraction of a second, registered the thought that he looked so wonderful that it didn't bear thinking about, and then she asked, with deliberate bluntness, 'What do you want?'

A slow, amused smile lifted the corners of Luke's mouth. He folded his arms and leant nonchalantly against the door-jamb. 'Ah, Robyn!' he drawled. 'Polite as always. I'm so glad you didn't disappoint me—just the greeting I expected. May I come in?'

Robyn narrowed her eyes. 'Don't you know what time——' she began, but already, somehow, he had moved past her into the dimly lit office and was standing confidently at her drawing-board, casually eyeing the plan that she had been working on. 'You work late,' he murmured, glancing around. 'Mmm, quite professional. Neat, too—something I hadn't expected.'

Robyn leant against the door to the office and found herself experiencing the old, familiar surge of deep annoyance. 'And I'm supposed to feel flattered,' she enquired waspishly, 'that you should deign to visit my humble office and actually compliment me on something?'

His mouth turned up lazily. 'If you like,' he replied, gazing at her with wicked amusement. 'After all, you already know just how rare my compliments are, don't you, Robyn? This will be the first. Although I do seem to remember a little scene after you'd carelessly cut your hand at the fountain, when I mentioned a few more personal attributes that were to my liking.'

'Was there some specific reason for this visit,' Robyn enquired, determinedly ignoring the teasing smile, the lurch in her stomach as her mind swung back to that morning. 'Or do you often make social calls at this hour of the night?'

'It has been known,' he informed her casually. 'Of course it all depends on the lady, on how well I know her. Believe it or not, Robyn, but some women are quite pleased to find me on their doorstep at midnight.'

I believe it! Robyn thought swiftly, moving further into the darker edges of the room, so that he wouldn't see too clearly how awful she looked. I do!

'Of course,' he continued swiftly, 'the reason I'm here, visiting you tonight, is quite different.'

That's it, Robyn thought irritably, rub it in! As if I don't feel bad enough already. Damn you, Luke! she muttered silently to herself. Turning up out of nowhere, catching me off guard like this, managing with the flick of an expression to make me feel inferior all over again!

'You left this, Robyn, at Paul and Melissa's house, after the party.' He reached into his pocket and produced her small black bag. 'They found it when they returned, and passed it on to me.'

'Oh! Oh, I see.' Robyn stepped forward reluctantly, moving into the pool of light to accept the bag he held out.

'So is business good?' he enquired, refusing to release the shiny bag, so that Robyn had to stand awkwardly in front of him in all her glorious finery and feel a hundred times worse than ever because his eyes were wandering over her face, travelling lazily down the length of her body, taking in every depressing detail.

'Reasonably,' Robyn murmured. 'I've been working hard——'

'Really?'

She flashed him a look. 'Yes, really! In fact,' she added smartly, 'I'm doing very well indeed! New projects, new clients.'

'Well, I'm pleased to hear that.'

There was a sparkle in his eyes, an amused expression on his face. No, you're not! Robyn thought. You couldn't care less, one way or the other—you just came here to have a little fun at my expense.

'Well, Robyn,' he smiled, 'as much as I would like to stay here, chatting with you until the small hours, I'm afraid I must be off. I've got quite a drive tonight.' He allowed her to take the bag and then brushed past and headed for the door. 'Thanks for the offer of coffee, Robyn, but I can't stay any longer——'

'Coffee?' Robyn repeated, without thinking. 'But I didn't. . . I mean. . .'

'Goodnight, Robyn,' he called laughingly, when he'd reached his car. 'Perhaps we'll have coffee another time! Don't work too hard, will you?'

Robyn stood at the open door and glared furiously as he got into his car and reversed away. She turned and looked down at the handbag, clutched tightly in her hand, and flung it far across the room. 'Arrogant swine!'

she muttered, as she switched off the light and climbed the stairs to her flat. 'Arrogant, arrogant swine!'

Saturday started surprisingly well. Robyn rose early to skies that promised a truly blissful day of warm summer sunshine, showered and dressed and then drove off in her dilapidated jeep which was packed to the gunwales with everything she might possibly need for the day ahead.

She even hummed along with the radio as she rattled down the motorway, something she hadn't felt like doing in a long time.

Gardening, from the first thought, to the planning on paper, to the actual satisfying sheer hard labour of it; that was her life. Robyn adored the way beautiful living pictures could be created outdoors with just some foresight and imagination and a knowledge of simple plants. It had been a slow process, of course, but gradually her reputation had grown and she had gained a singular name for creative, imaginative work. A warm glow of pride settled itself whenever she thought about it—her own business; she just wished her parents were still alive to witness it, and Mark, of course. . .

She brushed away the dullness that settled itself on her whenever she thought too hard about his death, about the way he had chosen to live parts of his life, the worries that had been there within her, deep below the surface, and forced herself to concentrate on finding the right numbered exit to this magnificent part of Gloucestershire.

Today, she decided, would be the start of something new; this client liked her work, must have, to choose her from among many possible designers. She would create something special, something outstanding for her. She had sounded so nice on the phone, not knowledgeable but pleasantly enthusiastic. It would be a pleasure.

It was an hour later that the jeep, always a vehicle that threatened trouble, started to sound distinctly unhappy. It would proceed perfectly well for a while and then suddenly lose all power, forcing Robyn to jerk and stutter along in first gear, while huge juggernauts and tractors hounded her from behind and threw her into a panic. Then the trouble would disappear and Robyn would heave a sigh of relief and smile at her luck, only to find the same thing happening a couple of miles down the road, and always after she'd passed a garage or a phone box.

It was a slow, infuriating process, and as A roads gave way to B and Robyn neared her destination already two hours late, the slowly darkening skies became as black and as desperate as Robyn's frame of mind, until the heavens opened and it started to pour—not reasonable, perfectly acceptable drops of rain from a warm July sky, but pounding, penetrating torrents that battered and bounced off the roof of the jeep and seeped in through the ill-fitting windows.

'Come on! Please! We're almost there,' Robyn pleaded aloud as she peered through the rain-soaked windscreen, between the wipers that were belting furiously back and forth as if their lives depended on it. 'Just get me to this place and then I can phone a garage. Please.'

The jeep continued to bounce and surge along the rutted, forlorn track that led, Robyn prayed, to the barn and to help, for several more minutes, while she gripped the wheel and perched on the edge of her seat, peering through the rain for any signs of civilisation.

And then it happened. With one last defiant surge of power the jeep finally gave up the ghost.

Robyn banged her hand on to the steering-wheel, cursing violently as she did so, and then slumped despondently with her head on her arms for a moment and lived her only recurring nightmare—that one day she would be stranded in some unknown place in the pouring rain in this damned broken-down wreck of a jeep with no one to help her.

She sat for maybe ten minutes staring gloomily out at the rain, which gave no sign of abating, knowing her options were limited to a choice of one. She would have to get out and walk. There was no getting away from it. But in this weather? It wasn't an attractive option, especially as she didn't need to glance behind at the carefully packed boot full of vital equipment to know that she had brought no waterproof coat; she was an optimist by nature and one with no foresight, always a lethal combination.

Finally and with a great sigh, Robyn forced herself into action. She couldn't carry on sitting in the comparative warmth of the jeep in the middle of nowhere, in the hope that a helpful garage man—or woman; she wasn't choosy—might happen by. She would just have to get out and walk.

Her jeans and shirt were soaked in less than three minutes. She thrust her hands into her pockets, bent her head and battled through the driving rain. It was slow progress. The rain, whipped up by the wind, bit into her face, stung the softly tanned skin on her neck and then trickled down the inside of her blouse, to merge with the hundred other rivulets of water that soaked into her skin.

The track seemed to go on forever. The once beautiful countryside began to appear hatefully menacing and the leaden skies, black with seemingly endless rain, hung low over the hills. A complete feeling of misery swept over Robyn, mixed with just a hint of panic, as she really began to despair that she had read her own instructions correctly and would never reach the barn or even civilisation again.

What would she do if there was no barn, no help? She could end up walking for miles, with no sign of anyone. She put the thought out of her mind, and forced herself to march harder, peering determinedly through the rain for any signs of life, almost willing the barn to appear——

Until finally, after ten minutes of desperate plodding, the welcome sight of a cream stone building arose around the next bend, nestled among a clump of very wet, but suddenly beautiful, rich green trees.

Robyn almost whooped with relief. She squelched through the mud at a half-trot and hoped with all her heart that someone, after all this agony, would be in; a kind, exceptionally friendly family would be nice; the elder son could be a brilliant mechanic and would mend her jeep with the proverbial wave of his spanner, the mother could be a fantastic cook. Robyn was starving.

She followed a makeshift, stepping-stone path, through a rapidly deepening quagmire of mud which led to the front door, and knocked loud and firm upon the solid oak panels.

It was a shame that she looked such a mess—this was hardly the best way to meet a prospective client—but once she'd explained her predicament. . .well, then everything would be all right. She had at least reached her destination.

The door opened and Robyn fixed her smile, prepared to launch into her quickly rehearsed explanation. But her smile froze, the explanation faltered on her lips.

She looked up into Luke's face and wondered why on earth she should be imagining him, here, now of all times. He was the last person in the world she wanted to see.

'Hello! You're late.' The mouth curled into an annoyingly attractive smile. 'And extremely wet. What happened this time? Not another fountain, surely?'

Robyn closed her mouth and swallowed and then swallowed again. 'You!' She wondered if she really could hallucinate a walking, talking nightmare. It couldn't really be him. God, no! Robyn struggled in the driving rain to keep a hold of her composure. 'What on earth are. . .?'

'Am I doing here?' he finished. 'Come on in out of the rain—you're absolutely drenched—and then I'll tell you.'

He opened the door wide and gestured for Robyn to enter as if it were the most natural thing in the world.

How can he? How can he have the nerve to stand there calm and composed and expect me to behave in the same way? she thought angrily.

She stayed exactly where she was, despite the rain, despite the inviting interior of the converted barn, glimpsed through the open door. No way was she falling in with his plans as easily as that! 'We can talk out here,' she told him stiffly. 'I'd like an explanation. I came here to see a Mrs Denner, to design her garden.'

His smile broadened, and she had to fight to concentrate on what he was saying. 'Yes, I know. Look, are you going to do the sensible thing for once and come in out of the rain? My hallway's getting soaked.'

It wasn't a request. Before Robyn knew what was happening he had taken hold of her arm and with one swift movement had pulled her inside, closing the door against the pouring rain, and dreary, foreboding skies.

'How dare you?' Robyn snapped. 'I don't know what sort of a game you're playing here but unless you tell me exactly why you've had me drive all the way down to this God-forsaken place I'm going straight back through that door!' She glared up at him. 'Don't laugh! I mean every word!'

'Oh, I know you do,' he said, straightening his face. 'I apologise for laughing, but you must admit it is rather amusing. What is it with you and water?'

She continued to glare up at him. 'Oh, well, I'm glad you find this all so amusing,' she snapped with heavy sarcasm. 'But it's no joke from where I'm standing. Having a vehicle break down and then struggling a mile down that pot-holed strip of mud you call a road isn't my idea of fun, I can tell you!'

'It's hardly my fault your car broke down,' he replied calmly.

'Never mind my breakdown!' Robyn retorted quickly. 'I want to know what you're doing here. Where's Mrs Denner? She phoned me earlier this week and invited me to come down here to see her land. The last person I expected to come across was you.'

'Yes,' he agreed. 'Your face just now was a picture of the most absolute astonishment.'

'Well?' Robyn's patience was beginning to wear thin. She was extremely wet and cold and the very last thing she needed was this man's mockery. 'Look, are you going to give me an explanation or not? Because if not I think I'd better be going.'

He lifted an enquiring eyebrow. 'Where to? I thought your vehicle had broken down. There's no other house around here for miles.'

Robyn swallowed and allowed her shoulders to sag.

This couldn't be happening, could it? Life surely couldn't be quite so cruel. Stranded here with this man?

'There's no need to look so desperate,' he replied with just a hint of sympathy. 'I will explain. First I'm afraid I do have to admit to a bit of deception on my part.'

I knew it! Robyn thought. This is all a horrible trick. But why? To punish me? she thought swiftly. Surely not! Surely this man wouldn't take his prejudices to such extremes.

'You see, there is no Mrs Denner,' he continued. 'I invented her. There's just me—Luke. Luke Denner.'

It suited him, the name, she thought. It had a strong, masculine ring about it. Hell, what am I thinking that for? Robyn cried silently. At a time like this! 'So what are you telling me? That I spoke to a figment of my imagination?' she snapped.

He gave a half-smile. 'No. She's my secretary. I asked her to phone because I thought you might just recognise my voice and as we didn't part on the best of terms. . .' He shrugged carelessly. 'The rest is all perfectly simple. You're a garden designer—a fact brought to my attention just a few weeks ago, if you remember; I want a garden designed.' He folded his arms and looked casually at her. 'So does that cause a problem.'

A problem? Was he still playing some kind of macabre joke? Did he really expect her to smile now and fall in with his plans, treat all this deception as no more than an unusual diversion? 'Of course there's a problem!' Robyn snapped. 'Working for you is a problem.'

'I don't see why,' he remarked. 'This is a genuine offer of work, no strings attached.'

'And I'm supposed to feel better now you've said that?' Robyn demanded. 'Never mind that I've been tricked, deceived into coming all the way down here! I should turn round and go straight back this minute!'

He leant across her and abruptly opened the door. 'No one is stopping you. Don't let it be said I kept you here against your will.'

Robyn swallowed and glanced out at the pouring rain, glanced at him, at the carved, arrogant profile that irked and thrilled her all at the same time and then at the rain again. Damn! She no more wanted to trudge all the way back to her jeep than she wanted to stay here arguing with this infuriating man. 'But I can't leave. My jeep's broken down.'

'Precisely,' he said curtly. 'So can I shut the door? Or do you plan to make a quick exit?'

'You can close it for the moment,' Robyn said reluctantly, 'until I've decided what to do.'

'Thank you,' he murmured drily.

'Now I'd like to know why me? I mean there are plenty of established designers around the country; you could have chosen any one of them.' She hardened her voice, remembering. 'And, as you've already said, we didn't part on the best of terms. In fact you made it perfectly plain from the very first moment just what you thought of me. Childish and irresponsible were two of your favouite adjectives—remember?'

Remember? she thought to herself. How could I forget? Every denigrating last phrase has been indelibly engraved in my memory. 'So, ' she continued, 'surely I'm the last person you think capable of completing this job?'

His mouth curled without amusement. 'Yes, you may be right. Frankly my doubts are increasing by the minute. This little entrance of yours hardly inspires professional confidence, does it? But then what have I to lose? My insatiable curiosity will be satisfied one way or the other and, as you said yourself, there are plenty of established garden designers I can call up if, or rather when, they're required.'

'So,' Robyn enquired, striving to keep her temper under control, 'you brought me all the way down here just so you could satisfy your own perverse curiosity?'

His lips curved into an infuriating smile. 'Yes, put like that, I suppose I did.'

'And you expect me to work for you, knowing you have not one ounce of faith in my abilities as a landscape designer?'

He looked at her pointedly. 'I don't expect anything. But what I am doing is giving you the opportunity to prove me wrong. This is a genuine project and one that

I would like to be completed before the end of the summer. You can take it or leave it. It's up to you.' He glanced down at Robyn's feet. 'Look, you're making a mess all over the floor. We'll talk later. Go upstairs now and get out of those clothes. Have a shower—you must be frozen.' His lips curved into a predatory smile and Robyn felt the uncontrollable twist of excited panic deep inside. 'Sounds rather familiar, doesn't it?'

'You're ordering me around again, if that's what you mean,' she replied, 'and if you think I'm going to trot obediently upstairs and take off all my clothes you must take me for a fool.'

He raised his eyebrows and smiled wickedly. 'You did it before; where's the difference?'

'There's a world of difference and you know it!' Robyn snapped.

'You mean this time you're sober?' he enquired silkily. 'But you're just as cold, and,' he added pointedly, 'continuing to tread mud all over a rather expensive Turkish rug—one that I'm particularly fond of.'

'Good!' Robyn snapped, glancing down at her wellingtons and the mud-stained tapestry of colours which covered the polished floor. 'Then my journey's not been totally wasted, has it?'

He sighed, 'Robyn, you're acting like a juvenile again. I expect rather more from my garden designers.'

'Funny. I didn't think you expected anything from this one! And besides I haven't said I'll take the job yet!'

'Well, then. It looks as if it's make-your-mind-up time, doesn't it? Don't waste my time, Robyn. Yes or no, it's as simple as that.'

Robyn glared at him. Waste his time! That was rich coming from him! She'd gone through agonies to get here and now. Damn it all! She had wanted this job so much too—needed it, if she was honest. A design on this sort of scale would be worth ten times the run-of-the-mill jobs she had completed just recently. She needed a change too, a new challenge. The prospect of designing among nature rather than battling with cement and glass and housing estates appealed enormously. She could do wonders here, turn the area around this beautifully designed barn into something special.

Oh, but this man! How could she work for him? Infuriating, arrogant, obnoxious, disbelieving. That was what stung most of all—the fact that he didn't even expect her to complete the one thing she loved doing in all the world, the one thing she was good at. No, not just good, brilliant! The silence lengthened. Robyn could see the impatience creeping into his face. 'It's going to cost a great deal of money. If you want a half-hearted approach I may as well not start in the first place.'

He raised his eyebrows. 'Is that your gracious way of accepting?' he asked drily.

Still time to back out, Robyn thought. Still time to walk away. There's no need to suffer this infernal man. There would be other gardens, other chances to prove her worth. But of course that was what hooked her. How could she let him get away with all he had said? All that he thought of her? If she were totally honest she would admit that over these last few weeks there had always been the memory of that party, the memory of him, his hostility, his unjustness. His kiss. Wasn't this what she had secretly hoped for? The chance at last to prove him wrong? To gain respect in this infuriating but somehow compelling man's eyes?

Robyn heard the rain, imagined its sheen of wetness on the grass, on the trees and plants, and found herself nodding slowly.

She had accepted the challenge. She would prove him wrong whatever happened.

CHAPTER FOUR

'THAT's settled, then. Take off your wellingtons and follow me.' Luke moved through a doorway that lead off from the right of the hallway and disappeared from view. Robyn stared after him and heaved a furious sigh. This was never going to work! Did he really expect her to trot right on after him—like an obedient dog or something?

A moment later and he had reappeared, powerful arms folded across the expanse of muscular chest, with a by now familiar look of resigned impatience. 'Are you going to stand there all afternoon?' he enquired. 'You do, presumably, want to get out of those wet things before you start work?'

Robyn met his gaze and forced herself to stay inert. One, two, three, four. . .she counted silently. . .and. . . five. Then she bent, casually, unhurriedly, and removed her boots, placed them carefully by the door and straightened up. She looked across and noted the twitch of a derisive smile, hovering near the edges of his mouth.

'Am I supposed to be impressed by this little bit of unhurried pantomime?' he enquired coolly. 'A bit late in the day, don't you think, for calm and composure?'

She glared at him. 'This is the way it's going to be from now on, Mr Denner,' she snapped, adding icy emphasis to his name. 'You have no respect for me—I can see that. . .'

'Hardly surprising,' he murmured with a derisive smile. 'The start of our professional relationship has been rather inauspicious, to say the least.'

'But I'm a businesswoman in my own right,' Robyn continued determinedly, doing her best to ignore his mocking expression. 'A reasonably successful one. So if you imagine that orders and irritation are going to intimidate me you're in for a big surprise! Other people may be frightened by your blunt arrogance, but don't

make the mistake of including me in that category. . .
I——'

'Quit gabbling, woman. If I were you I'd save my
breath and my energy for later—talking never proved a
thing; it's actions that count. And I'm afraid that as all
I've seen is one miscalculated mishap after another
you've got an awful long way to go before I'm convinced
of anything. Now, why don't you just go upstairs like a
good little girl and get out of those wet things? After
that maybe, just maybe, you can start proving to me you
do possess some measure of professionalism—although
to be honest,' he added caustically, 'I'm finding it hard
to believe you're capable of distinguishing between a
weed and an orchid at the moment, or even digging a
garden, let alone ever designing one.'

She went, with a glare at Luke Denner that would
have turned a lesser man to stone. What else was there
to do? she thought miserably as she squelched behind
him up to the bathroom. She resembled a particularly
pathetic drowned rat, hardly a solid rock from which to
argue her case—and he was enjoying every minute of it.
Besides, he held all the cards, and so far, she thought
dejectedly, she had played right into his hands.

Robyn hugged herself dry with a warm towel. Déjà vu
was one thing, she thought irritably, but this was bor-
dering on the ridiculous! She still couldn't quite believe
that all this *was* actually happening to her. If somebody
had told her she'd find herself in this same dubious
position all over again, even one hour ago, she would
have laughed right in their face. Me? she would have
laughed. Let myself fall into that trap again? Well, who
was it who had the last laugh now?

So full of hope, so cheerful this morning—a new start!
she thought. 'You don't deserve this, Robyn, my girl,'
she muttered mournfully at her misted reflection. 'Not
at all. It's a cruel twist of fate, that's what it is.'

She grabbed the ubiquitous towelling robe from the
hook on the door and wrapped it almost angrily around
her body. What on earth have I agreed to work for him
for? she asked herself despairingly. I know he'll reject all

my plans and ideas for the garden out of hand, just to prove a sadistic point. I'm a fool if I believe for one minute that he'll give me a fair chance. . .

The robe was his. The scent of his cologne, discreet and expensive, wafted upwards, alerting her senses, halting her thoughts in their tracks. Robyn pressed her face against the soft navy towelling and breathed in deeply, slowly, allowing the wonderful scent to pervade completely her senses.

Of course it's his! she told herself crossly, after a moment. Why ever not? This is his house, his bathroom after all! Still, it was particularly unnerving, somehow, to find her naked body so closely enfolded in a garment that had done the very same thing for him—strange, personal, intimate.

'Have you finished?'

Robyn started at the sound of his voice. 'Umm—yes.' She cleared her throat. 'Yes, just about.'

'Well, if you give me the keys to the jeep, I'll go and take a look at it for you—get anything you might need.'

Robyn checked the mirror, made sure no flesh was visible from the neck down, drew back the bolt and opened the door. Remembering at the last minute her policy of poise and control, she straightened up and formed what she hoped was a suitably businesslike expression. 'Here you are.' She handed him the keys from her jeans, careful to avoid his touch. 'There's a large holdall with all my equipment, if you could get that—please,' she added reluctantly.

'OK. Anything else?'

Robyn shook her head. 'No, unless you think you might be able to fix it?' she asked hopefully, as he turned away. 'I mean, it could be something incredibly simple, couldn't it?'

'I'm not planning to stay long enough to find out— have you see the rain? It's worse than ever,' he returned. 'Consider yourself lucky that I'm offering to get your things.'

'Helpful sort of a swine, aren't you?' Robyn snapped sarcastically.

He gave a cool, unhurried smile. 'Let's just say I'm

about as helpful as you are practical—it wouldn't surprise me if you hadn't just run out of petrol.'

'Don't be ridiculous!' Robyn retorted. 'Even I can look at a gauge and make out when it's on the red!'

'Unless it's broken,' he replied. 'It has been known.'

'It is *not* broken! I know. It is my jeep, for God's sake!'

He raised his eyebrows and gave her a cool stare. 'It was only a suggestion, Robyn; there's no need to blow a fuse.'

'Well, it's a pretty stupid suggestion. I'm not half-witted, you know; I can read and write and work things out for myself!'

His lips curved again, just to make her extra mad, a derisive, superior smile that none the less transformed his features wonderfully and made Robyn's heart leap and turn, despite her irritation. 'No, of course you're right,' he declared sarcastically. 'Why on earth would I ever think to question your ability? Practical common sense—they're your watchwords, aren't they? How else would you get into the marvellous position that you find yourself in now?' He threw the keys casually up into the air and caught them. 'So do you want some coffee?'

Robyn glared; how she longed to wipe that infuriating smile off his face!

'Coffee?' she snapped. 'I'm supposed to be content with that? What about a change of clothes, a mended jeep?'

A magic fairy that would whisk her away from all this, she thought, who could turn the clock back and give her a second chance—a more dignified entrance perhaps, a way of showing this arrogant rat just what she thought of him. Coffee!

'OK, please yourself. But I could do with one,' he drawled. 'You can make yourself useful while I'm gone; there's a percolator in the kitchen—I like mine strong and black.'

'With or without arsenic?' Robyn shouted, as he descended the spiral staircase and crossed the enormous living-room below.

She stared furiously after him, waited until she heard

the thud of the front door, the low throaty rumble of his Range Rover, and then she gave vent to a screech of frustration—short, sharp and extremely satisfying.

He was away no more than five minutes.

The Range Rover's lights swept into view, illuminating the torrents of rain, the unusually dark, almost eerie gloom. Robyn watched from the shelter of the long cream curtains which shrouded the vast downstairs window, her finger curled thankfully around the mug of hot, hot coffee. Good. He was wet, despite the long waxed raincoat. His hair, darkened by the rain, clung to his head, his smooth, tanned face glistened with its sheen of moisture. Perhaps, if she was lucky, droplets would, at this very moment, be dripping uncomfortably down his neck, finding their way insidiously downwards, chilling his warm skin, soaking his nice dry shirt.

She watched as he made a run for the barn, her holdall, cumbersome and heavy, in one hand, across the stepping-stones, the mud, the quagmire that would, if Robyn had her way, soon become a large paved terrace. A small smile of satisfaction slipped into place. She treasured it—probably the only smile she'd get all day. Oh, yes, he was wet all right! The rain bounced and splattered and visibly stung him with its force.

A few moments later and he came in, coat removed, a towel draped casually around his neck, rubbing vigorously at his hair with strong, tanned fingers. She watched him nervously and then he casually stretched up and removed his damp shirt so that it took all her powers, her resolutions, to appear composed in sight of his taut, powerful torso. That will teach me, she thought, for wishing him wet.

'Your holdall's in the kitchen,' he murmured casually. 'What have you got in that thing? It weighs an absolute ton.'

'Just my equipment,' Robyn replied smartly. 'I saw you struggling with it; you should have left it in the Range Rover—I would have lifted it out for you.'

She saw his look, the way his mouth twisted into a smile, and then he was moving towards her, every sculptured muscle on his chest and arms rippling with quite obvious power. 'Don't be provocative, Robyn,' he murmured, lifting her chin towards him with one light touch of his finger. 'You may find it results in more than you can handle.'

Robyn swallowed and took a hasty pace backwards, struggling desperately against the compelling strength of his gaze, the overwhelming male sexuality that exuded from him. 'I. . . I don't suppose you looked at the jeep while you were there?' she murmured croakily, just for something to say.

'No.' He backed off with a satisfied twist of his mouth. 'Not that I would have been able to do much anyway, that thing's a death trap! Someone would need to be a genius to get that pile of rust going; you forgot to mention it was a complete and utter wreck—I'm surprised it got you this far!'

Robyn had thought much the same on numerous occasions but she wasn't about to give him the satisfaction of letting him know that. 'Well, I'm sorry if it doesn't meet with your approval, Mr Denner,' she snapped icily, 'but we can't all afford brand-new Range Rovers!'

'Who mentioned anything about brand-new Range Rovers?' he enquired evenly. 'Anything would have to be an improvement on that pile of junk!'

'Well, thank you very much for your expert opinion, but that "death trap", as you call it, is the only vehicle I happen to possess and I need it mended pretty quickly. So,' she enquired haughtily, putting down her coffee-mug with a flourish, 'would it be too much trouble to ask for the number of the nearest garage? I think it's time I did something about getting out of this damnable situation.'

He draped the towel around his shoulders and shook his head. ''Fraid I can't help you, Robyn,' he said with a sarcastic smile. 'Owners of brand-new Range Rovers don't have a lot of call for tow-trucks and the like.'

She might have known he would be less than helpful. 'Well, where's the phone, then—I am allowed to use it, I presume?'

He nodded towards the kitchen. 'Go ahead; you'll be wasting your time, of course.'

'Don't be ridiculous!' Robyn declared. 'The jeep's not that bad. Besides,' she added caustically, 'I don't believe you know a thing about engines anyway!'

She noted the flicker of a smile as he came into the kitchen and poured himself a cup of coffee, but she ignored him, turning her back as she scanned the phone book, desperately hunting for a garage that was reasonably near to this god-forsaken place. There didn't seem to be many at all. Eventually, though, she found a number that looked at least hopeful and began dialling. Damn! No answer. She tried another and another, until finally the receiver was firmly removed from her grasp and replaced back on its cradle.

'What do you think you're doing?' she cried angrily, spinning round.

'Saving you time,' he murmured. 'There's no one about; haven't you worked that out yet?'

'But it's only just gone four o'clock!' Robyn exclaimed. 'Of course there someone about!'

'I'm afraid you're going to be disappointed, Robyn. This is the country—the real country, not deepest suburbia. When I said it would be a waste of time, I wasn't referring to the state of your jeep.' He shrugged with obvious unconcern and took a mouthful of coffee, 'Saturday afternoons are dead, just like Sundays. Anywhere after one o'clock and you've had it. Nothing. Finished.'

'But surely the garages must have an emergency service or something?' Robyn replied with just an edge of panic in her voice.

'Not around here, they don't. Of course with a wreck like you've got you should be in one of the big motoring organisations—that way you wouldn't be in this situation now.' He paused. 'You aren't, I suppose? No,' he added with an infuriating smile, 'I thought not.'

'So what am I supposed to do?' Robyn asked, just a little shakily as her mind raced ahead to the possibilities before her and then retreated with equal speed, because her mind didn't like what it saw. 'I can't just sit here stranded.'

He shrugged and then he laughed, his teeth gleaming white against the tanned, swarthy skin of his face. 'There's no need to look so panic-stricken, Robyn. Don't worry, your wreck will be mended. First thing Monday morning and we'll call again; someone will come out then as good as gold.'

'Monday?' Robyn wailed incredulously. 'But I can't wait till then! That's out of the question! What am I supposed to do in the meantime?'

'Work for me, of course,' he snapped. 'That was the general idea, wasn't it? Unless you're backing out, of course. . .'

She looked at him defiantly. 'I'm not backing out. . .but. . .but. . .'

'But what? You can stay the weekend.'

Robyn stared at him aghast. 'Stay the weekend? Here? With you?'

'You're repeating everything I say, Robyn.'

'That's because I can't believe what I'm hearing,' she shot back. 'You don't honestly expect me to agree to that idea?'

'I don't see you have a great deal of choice,' he drawled, 'unless of course you wish to walk home—in which case you may as well forget our agreement. A garden designer who doesn't wish to look at her garden is of no use to me. If you're sensible and serious about wanting this opportunity, you'll start work tomorrow—measure up, take notes. . .'

'Will you stop telling me how to do my job?' Robyn snapped. 'I know how to run my own business. I know what's involved!'

'Good, then you'll know that time is money and the client's satisfaction is everything. This arrangement, as far as I can see, scores well on both counts.'

'Well, it doesn't score points with me!' Robyn muttered. 'I am not happy.'

He threw her a cool, unperturbed look. 'No, I can see that. Personally, I think you should be counting your lucky stars.' His lips curled into what was unmistakably a predatory smile. 'You could have, after all, been stranded with someone you'd never set eyes on—someone who wasn't the least bit hospitable. Aren't you relieved you're in this situation with a familiar face? After all,' he added provokingly, 'this is old ground; we've gone through this before, haven't we?'

Robyn's eyes narrowed furiously. 'You're really enjoying this, aren't you?' she snapped.

'It has its attractions,' he agreed. 'Seeing you fighting to control your temper is quite entertaining, I'll admit. Tut-tut, Robyn, you disappoint me, you really do. Don't I get any thanks for offering to put you up for the weekend?'

Robyn looked at him and flirted with the idea of telling him where to get off. Arrogant swine! 'And. . .and what about the sleeping arrangements?' she asked stiffly, hugging the robe which suddenly felt far too flimsy, close around her body.

'I have a guest bedroom, don't worry,' he replied lazily. 'So what honour and reputation you do possess will be totally uncompromised.'

'And what exactly do you mean by that?' she snapped.

'Exactly what I say,' he growled, looking her straight in the eyes. 'What honour and reputation you possess will not be compromised.'

The party. Of course! Robyn thought angrily. He still remembers, still won't let me forget. Still looks upon me as a. . .as a——

'Well, now we've sorted out your little problem,' he continued briskly, interrupting Robyn's hazy memory of that totally forgettable fiasco, 'what about more mundane matters? Food for instance—are you hungry?'

She was. Absolutely starving. But a perversity born out of irritation and anger, with him, with the whole damn situation, made her snap, 'No. I am not! I couldn't eat a thing.'

He shrugged indifferently, making her immediately regret her stupidity; she really could die for some good hot food!

'OK, fine. I'm going to get out of these damp clothes and then I've got some phone calls to make.' He put his mug down on the draining-board. 'We'll eat later—make yourself at home till then.'

She watched him leave the kitchen, sighed furiously and then stared blankly into space. Make yourself at home! Who was he kidding? No clothes, no food, no friendly face and no way of escape!

She wandered back into the living-room, with its rugged stone walls and polished wood and leather, and looked out again at the darkened skies and pouring rain. What should she do, stranded here like this? Oh, God! It was all so frustrating, infuriating. If she didn't know better she'd have said he'd sabotaged her jeep and made it rain this way, just so he could enjoy some amusement at her expense!

Do I want this job so badly? she asked herself for the hundredth time. Is it really worth all this. . .this aggravation and humiliation? She thought seriously for a moment, considering. But even if she declined now, what would she do? Her jeep was blocking that infernal track completely, so until a tow-truck did turn up there was no way out anyway! She was stuck here, it seemed, for good or bad, until Monday, just as he'd said.

I'll phone Anne, she thought suddenly, tell her what's going on; the sound of her voice will make me feel better—she might even have an idea.

She didn't know what it was, but once on the phone she couldn't bring herself to tell Anne all the miserable details. It would take too long and she wouldn't understand; besides, she had phoned at a bad moment—Anne was obviously in a hurry to go out.

'So I'll see you Monday, then?' Anne said cheerfully. 'Have a nice weekend down in the country, you lucky thing!'

Lucky! Robyn put the phone down morosely and felt a shiver run the length of her body. If only Anne could see her now, dressed as she was, knew the sort of man she was having to put up with!

She wrapped the gown close around her body and wandered back into the living-room, moving around aimlessly, pausing in front of the enormous bookcase that virtually filled one large section of the room from top to bottom. His library was well stocked. Dickens, Shakespeare, Thackeray, Shaw; either he was deliberately out to impress, which she reluctantly doubted, or he really was well read. She took down a couple of volumes, flicked through them, placed them back. It was no good; reading at this moment in time was the last thing she felt like. It was taking all her powers of concentration just to keep warm.

Her clothes! What on earth was she thinking of? They were hardly going to get dry, just draped upstairs in the bathroom. There was a tumble-drier in the kitchen; she had seen it when she'd gone in there to call Anne. Fifteen minutes in that thing should see them wonderfully dry, surely?

She bounded upstairs, her bare feet silent on the cast-iron staircase, and pushed open one of the three identical wooden doors that led off from the galleried landing.

Wrong door. Too late she saw that—about a fraction of a second after seeing Luke Denner naked, except for the briefest of underpants, standing in front of a wardrobe, pulling a pair of jeans from a hanger. Robyn knew she was staring, knew her eyes had already travelled the length of his incredible muscular body, assessed every inch of powerful physique, before he realised she was there.

He looked up and saw her and Robyn blushed furiously, fixed to the spot with embarrassment. 'Like what you see?' he enquired, eyebrows raised in lazy amusement. 'Well?' he persisted, and then he laughed. 'What's the matter, Robyn, haven't you seen a man's body this close before? You're still staring,' he added teasingly. 'Haven't you learned that it's not very polite?'

'I wasn't,' Robyn muttered. 'I mean. . . I . . . I opened the door by mistake; I'm looking for the bathroom, my clothes. . .'

'I'll believe you,' he said carelessly, pulling on his jeans, fastening the buttons at his waist, 'although millions wouldn't. I thought for a minute you had that look about you.'

'Look?' Robyn queried awkwardly, averting her eyes from the feast of muscle, the dark, dark hair that travelled from his chest down and down. . .He pulled on a worn denim shirt but refrained from buttoning it, so that his gorgeous chest was still visible, still reminding her. . .

'Yes, you know——' he turned and faced her, rough, tanned, virile, full of masculine sexuality and his lips twitched '—the look of a woman hungry for the sight of a man's body!'

Robyn blushed deep cerise and glared, making sure her look was as unhungry as she could make it, and dived for the handle of the other door.

Robyn hugged her arms around her body. She had been watching the tumble-drier for ages and still her clothes weren't quite dry. She wandered back into the living-room. The door at the far end of the room, which she presumed was his study, was still closed, but she could hear the muffled sound of his voice and—surprise, surprise!—even the sound of a relaxed laugh. So he was capable of genuine humour, then, Robyn thought bitterly, not just sarcasm and mockery!

Her eyes fell to the open fireplace, the large, gaping grate with its neat pile of sawn logs. She stared thoughtfully for a moment or two. Make yourself at home, he had said. Well, damn him, she would! What was the point in suffering like this? He obviously couldn't give a damn what she did, tucked away in his cosy room, dressed in his nice dry clothes. Five minutes later and after exploration in all the kitchen cupboards, Robyn had found matches, and some old newspapers. She sat back on her heels and watched with pleasure as the flames surged and roared and the twigs sparked and crackled up into the wide opening of the chimney. It was a good blaze. She stretched her hands out and warmed them thankfully, remembering those happier times when, as children, she and Mark had argued about the best way to light a fire, had helped their mother after many disheartening attempts with damp wood and wet coal. It had been a special childhood, full of laughter and fun; Mark and she had grown up together as friends, as well as brother and sister. Robyn blinked back unexpected tears and leant forward to place a log carefully on to the mound of hot red twigs. She shouldn't be thinking of him now, not here, not like this. It was too stupid of her to let the memories come crowding in so easily.

She swallowed back the lump in her throat and looked at the fire. What was wrong with the damn thing? Smoke was billowing outwards, choking plumes of the stuff. Robyn scrambled back out of the way and watched helplessly as the choking greyness filled the room. 'Oh, crikey!' she muttered, glancing fearfully towards the study door. 'What on earth shall I do?' The smoke was getting worse, travelling at surprising speed across the room—she would have to do something.

'What the hell are you up to now?' Robyn caught sight of Luke's furious face as he strode across, and momentarily closed her eyes. 'For heaven's sakes,' he growled irritably, 'I can't leave you alone for five minutes, can I?'

Robyn coughed violently and wiped at her by now streaming eyes. 'It's not my fault!' she choked breathlessly. 'How was I to know the chimney would be blocked or whatever it is that's wrong with the thing? You said make yourself at home!'

'I didn't mean completely wreck the place! Look at this room!' He went out and returned a moment later with a metal bucket and spade. Robyn watched as he scraped the burning embers and logs into it. 'Open those french windows!' he ordered. 'Let's get some fresh air in here.'

He must have taken the bucket outside but when he returned Robyn was still struggling furiously with the unfamiliar catch.

'Leave it!' he commanded irritably. 'Just leave it and go into the kitchen. And for God's sake shut the door behind you or we'll have smoke everywhere.'

She fled. Angry, frustrated, humiliated—all the usual emotions experienced time and again in his presence. I should be used to it by now, she thought miserably. But she wasn't—not at all.

He came into the kitchen after a few moments and she turned away, wandering to the far side to get away from him, battling with the sudden incredible desire to

break down and sob like a little girl who had done the
wrong thing yet again.

'The smoke's dispersing.' He went over to the sink
and began washing his hands. 'Thank God all the
upstairs doors were closed, or the smell of smoke would
have been everywhere. Why didn't you tell me you were
cold, for heaven's sake? I would have lit the fire for you.'

She struggled to hold on to her composure, closing
her eyes against the tears. He would have to appear
now, wouldn't he—when she wasn't prepared? The
sound of running water ceased and she guessed he was
drying his hands.

'Well, now we've survived another of your mini-
disasters,' he continued, 'I thought that after dinner
we'd look at the plans; it will save time tomorrow. I've
got some ideas I'd like to discuss.' There was a pause.
'Robyn?'

Damn him! she thought miserably. Damn his ability
to act as if he hadn't just shouted like mad at her! She
squeezed her eyes shut and lowered her head, hiding
behind her curtain of auburn curls, battling with the
tears, battling with the fact that it mattered because she
had made a mistake again. She couldn't speak. The
tears were locked in her throat, tight and painful and
immovable.

'Oh, for God's sake!' She heard the sound of a towel
being slapped down irritably, the sigh of impatience.
'You're not going to sulk!'

I mustn't cry, she told herself. He mustn't see me cry.
It was her only concern. Never any tears in public; no
tears at all, if she could help it—but to cry in front of
him! It would be so humiliating, so weak.

She struggled, she really did struggle to say something, anything as long as he didn't see that she was
upset by his outburst of anger.

'You've brought this on yourself, Robyn. Don't be
childish,' he growled.

'Leave me alone!' she cried unsteadily. 'Just leave me
be! I'm sick of your orders and your. . .your temper. I'm
sick of everything,' she added bitterly, taking a huge

breath. 'I don't need you telling me how to behave. I just want to be left alone.'

'As you like,' he murmured and then, surprisingly, he left without another word. She heard the quiet click of the door and when she raised her head she had got what she wanted—she was alone.

Robyn let out a deep sigh and realised that she was shaking from head to foot. What's wrong with me? she thought. Why can't I handle this? Large, silent tears filled her eyes and trickled slowly down her cheeks. It was the strain—deep down she knew—the strain of finding herself in this diabolical situation, the strain of being alone here, like this, with his contempt and superiority, struggling constantly against the physical awareness of him, the electricity that his presence produced. He was draining her from every angle, mentally, physically and. . .and sexually. It was humiliating admitting as much, but she had never felt so attracted, so excited by the physical appearance of a man. Just being in the same room as him sent shivers of something down her spine that up to now she had never experienced. I won't name it, she thought determinedly, I won't even think it. But she knew what she felt and it shocked her.

Robyn heard his footsteps crossing the hall and she wiped furiously at her damp face with the sleeve of his gown, rushing to the door, pressing her body firmly against it. 'Don't come in!' she cried shakily, 'I'm getting dressed.'

'Robyn, are you OK?' She heard his voice, puzzled, suspicious, only inches away on the other side.

Deep breaths, now, Robyn, she told herself; come on, pull yourself together. . . One, two, three. Robyn swallowed, tried to steady her voice.

'Yes. Yes, of course I am. Why shouldn't I be? I just wanted to get dressed in peace. Is that too much to ask?'

'Not at all.' She registered the change of tone—hardened, icy, just like her own. 'Well, when you've finished, you can start working for your keep and begin dinner. I'm famished even if you're not. There's cold chicken and salad in the fridge. I'll leave you in absolute peace and get back to work!'

Robyn let out a sigh and closed her eyes with relief. That had been close—too close. She went over to the sink and splashed her face with cold water over and over again. Her jeans and shirt were dry now. She pulled them on hastily, half expecting Luke to come bursting in at any minute. She had snapped at him again, and this time, remarkably, she admitted that he hadn't deserved it. I must keep my cool, she thought; losing my temper, antagonising him like this isn't going to help my situation, is it? She would have to start remembering that he was a client. If she wanted this job, she would have to be reasonably pleasant to him, however much it stuck in her throat at times.

It was a pleasant, organised kitchen and the purpose of a regular, everyday task had a soothing, therapeutic effect on Robyn. Crusty bread and thick, creamy butter, a huge crisp salad, masses of succulent cold chicken; there was wine in the fridge too, as well as rows of the stuff in the extensive wine racks that lined one wall of the kitchen. Would it be too presumptuous to get a bottle out? Did he drink wine with his meals?

She was just debating when the door opened and he came in. The unexplainable spark of excitement, at being in his presence again, shocked her. She shouldn't feel this way—particularly when his opinion of her was so obvious. Yet nothing, it seemed, could halt the flow of adrenalin that surged upwards or the flush of awareness that overwhelmed her as he cast his eyes over the carefully laid table, the food and, lastly, herself.

He didn't look very happy, but then, when had she ever seen him look anything except cool or irritable, or arrogantly amused?

'I prefer to eat in the other room,' he announced briskly. 'I've unblocked the chimney; the fire's going well now.' He grabbed a tray from a cupboard and placed it on the table. 'Why haven't you got the wine out?' he asked tersely, opening the fridge door, 'I'll open this—you take the rest of the stuff through.'

Robyn bit her lip and half considered throwing the

whole lot over him. Somehow, against her better judgement, she refrained and placed his plate with chicken and salad on to the tray. So, he wished to eat alone! She obviously wasn't good enough to share a meal with! Well, that suited her—it suited her just fine!

He came through as she was slamming the food on to the low coffee-table in front of the obediently blazing fire. She could see the attraction of eating in here on an evening like this, apart from the one of getting away from her, of course. It really was very inviting, relaxing, with the warm brickwork, the soft glow from the lamps, the flickering fire. He placed the wine bottle and glasses on to the table beside her. Two glasses, she noticed suddenly.

'Where's yours?' he asked, surveying the one place setting. 'Aren't you eating?'

Robyn blushed. 'I . . . I thought you wanted to eat alone. I. . .'

He gave her a withering look. 'Don't be an idiot, girl! Go and get your plate in here now—I may be blunt, but I'm not a complete bastard!'

Robyn fetched her plate and self-consciously came back into the room. Luke watched her as she gingerly helped herself to some of the food. 'This is very nice, Robyn, thank you.'

She glanced across quickly—was he mocking again? Robyn studied his expression and felt surprised. No, it seemed not. 'It's just salad,' she mumbled, 'nothing very complicated.'

'Looks pretty wonderful to me,' he replied. 'I haven't eaten since breakfast.'

It was wonderful. Robyn sat on the floor by the fire, with her plate on her lap, and tucked in. And gradually, as the warmth and the food took its effect, she felt the stirrings of a new emotion, a first in his company. She glanced across at Luke, registering the strong line of his jaw, the slight indentation in his chin, the devastating blue of his eyes. Guilt. She had been rude earlier on and Robyn knew she should apologise. She did it before she could change her mind. 'I'm sorry about before,' she

murmured between mouthfuls. 'The fire. . .and everything; I didn't mean to snap so.'

His eyes met hers and it was a slow, thoughtful look.
'It's been one of those days, hasn't it, Robyn?' he
murmured evenly. 'Perhaps we've both been a little
affected by the way things have gone. I lost my temper
too—I'm sorry for shouting about the fire. I didn't mean
to upset you.'

'I. . . I. . .you didn't,' Robyn mumbled, totally confused by his unexpected apology. 'And you mean the
smoke,' she added lightly, 'not the fire—there was very
little flame.'

He flashed a sudden stunning smile and Robyn felt
weak as a new surge of exhilaration raced through her.
'You're right,' he replied. 'Well, let's forget it, shall we?
Just enjoy our meal.'

He poured the wine and Robyn gradually, inch by
inch, moment by moment, found herself slowly beginning to relax, to actually feel comfortable in her surroundings—something she would have thought
impossible only a few minutes ago. She leant lazily
against the sofa and they talked a little and ate and drank
and the evening progressed and Robyn found that, aston-
ishingly, she was enjoying herself, relaxing back against
the sofa, stretching out her long legs in front of her,
listening to the deep, magnetic timbre of his voice.

She placed her knife and fork on to her plate at last
and looked up to find his sparkling eyes upon her. 'So
what was all that earlier about not being hungry?' he
asked. 'I don't think I've ever seen anyone enjoy their
food so much!'

Robyn flushed deep scarlet. 'Was I an awful pig?' she
murmured. 'Sorry.' He smiled and Robyn watched and
felt her heart stop for the hundreth time.

'No need to apologise again, Robyn—twice in one
evening and I'll seriously start believing that there's
something wrong with you!' He took a mouthful of wine
and regarded her, propping one hand against his head.
'It's rather a change, actually,' he murmured, 'to find a
woman who doesn't pick at her food and moan about
endless diets. Almost every woman I've known had to

live off a perpetual menu of rabbit's food. It's a terrible appetite-killer, sitting opposite someone who picks and fiddles with their food, when all the time you're desperate to tuck in like a pig.'

'I couldn't diet,' Robyn declared, deliberately not allowing herself to imagine what all the women he had known would look like. 'It would be like hell. I love food too much.'

She saw his eyes skim reflectively over her body, felt herself blush under his potent male gaze. Then he brought his blazing eyes unhurriedly to her face and for a long moment she found herself wishing time would stand still; when he looked at her like that . . . she swallowed, felt her pulse beating wildly; his eyes were devouring hers. And then abruptly he looked away and said with neutral politeness, 'Would you like something else—some dessert perhaps? There's gâteau in the fridge, I think.'

There was, too. Thick and gooey and chocolatey. Robyn had already spotted and drooled over it earlier. 'No. No, thank you,' she replied regretfully. 'I'd better not. I don't want to appear too much of a glutton.'

'Well, I'll clear away, then. No, you stay here,' he instructed as Robyn made a move to help. 'You prepared the meal. I'll bring us in some coffee.'

It was amazing, she thought when he had left the room, what food, wine and a sensational smile could do for a girl. She had felt so scratchy and irritable before—not surprising, given the way the day had gone, but hardly fair, perhaps, to take it *all* out on him—— Most of it, she thought, smiling, yes.

Robyn stared dreamily into the flames. They were having an hypnotic effect, like Luke's voice, his eyes. She stretched lazily and made herself more comfortable. To be here as his special guest, she thought, wanted, invited for a totally different reason; how must that feel? To look across and see that gorgeous smile, find those brilliant eyes burning at you with desire and love, instead of derision and mockery.

She allowed herself the luxury of remembering the

way he had looked at her just now, thought about how she had felt.

A log rolled and half fell out of the grate, making Robyn jump suddenly. She reached across quickly and pushed it back and then sat up, shaking her head a little.

What am I doing, she thought incredulously, thinking this way? Am I mad or drunk? Or both perhaps? She shook her head in exasperation, remembering his deception and total lack of sympathy, the way he had treated her on that first night, that following morning. The wine—had she really allowed it to dim all her common sense, lull her into a false sense of security? Surely she hadn't almost fallen for the oldest trick in the book! Robyn remembered his free and easy hand as he had poured her wine. Was he really trying to get her drunk? He wouldn't dare, surely? she thought angrily. He wouldn't stoop so low!

He came back through then and she averted her eyes from the fire, and his face, and wandered over to the window, to sober herself by staring once again at the pouring rain.

'Here—some gâteau.' He joined her and held out a dish full of sponge and cream and morello cherries.

'I did say that I didn't want any,' Robyn declared coolly.

'Yes, I know.' He smiled—damn him, he smiled and it was wonderful. 'But you didn't mean it, did you?'

She wanted it to be friendly and relaxed as before, she wanted to laugh and joke with him, but it was out of the question now. She took the dish, and suppressed her normal automatic impulse to smile. 'Thank you,' she murmured. He watched her as she took a small mouthful of the delicious moist sponge. 'It's good,' she said, for something to say.

'I have a wonderful ladyfriend who stocks me up with food whenever I'm down here,' he replied. 'She made it.'

The sponge suddenly lost a little of its flavour. Ladyfriend? Yes, of course, he would have, wouldn't he? She was a good cook too. 'Oh, I see,' she murmured, thinking of her own diabolical culinary efforts. 'That's very convenient.' She paused and decided to change the subject. 'So you don't live here permanently, then?'

'Not at the moment, no,' he replied, taking a sip of coffee. 'I've got a flat in London for convenience. I've spent the last two years converting this place in my spare time; it's only recently been habitable enough to live in.'

Robyn glanced around the room, surprised, interested, despite her resolution to remain aloof and unimpressed from now on. 'You did the work yourself? Or do you mean you paid a lot of tradesmen to come in and do the work for you? There is a difference.'

'I had the help of a bricklayer and a carpenter from time to time, but no, in the main I did most of the work myself. It's been good for me to sweat and toil—like a long therapy session; honest manual work puts a lot of things in perspective. But then you would know about that—your business, that must have taken a fair amount of hard work.'

'Yes. Yes, it did,' she agreed. 'A great deal.'

'Worth it?' he asked interestedly. 'Worth all the hassle?'

Robyn nodded slowly, remembering fleetingly all the long hours, the struggles. 'Definitely. Hard at times, of course, frustrating too—there are always days when you wonder why you keep on struggling, keep on slogging away; but the pleasure of doing something you enjoy, of creating and knowing that it's all yours. . .' she shrugged '. . .well, there's nothing else like it.'

'You love your work.'

She looked at him. 'Of course,' she said simply. 'It's been everything to me, kept me sane, kept me going through all. . .' She stopped, embarrassed suddenly, looked down, realised with a start just how close she had been to revealing some parts of her life, her thoughts. . .

'I'm tired,' she announced suddenly—too suddenly— placing her dish, half-finished, on a table. 'I'm very tired and I need to get some sleep. I'll be up early in the morning.'

He was surprised, she could see that, by the change in her manner, her voice, the sudden swing in her mood. Well, it couldn't be helped. She had allowed him to come too close, to penetrate her defences far too easily as it was this evening. The only reason she had decided to put herself through all this with him was because she had a point to prove—a professional point. She must remember that.

Tomorrow she would be fresher, more able to deal with this disconcerting ability of his to disarm at will with a casual smile and a deceiving show of interest.

But not now. For at this moment, standing here beside him, part of her really wanted to believe in things that could never, ever be. And that surely was the quickest route to disaster.

CHAPTER FIVE

THE dawn chorus woke Robyn at five. By half-past, she had showered, dressed and crept past the door to his room and was outside in the fresh, sparkling air of a new day.

It was glorious! Such a relief to be among the long, wet grass and blue, blue skies, to feel free and alive, to be alone with her thoughts, unfettered, if only for a while, from the frustrations and restraints of yesterday.

She wandered, hands in jeans, hair pulled up into a workmanlike topknot, and simply enjoyed the rough, uncultivated feel of the land. Did Luke appreciate all this? she thought suddenly, watching as a rabbit lifted its head a moment and then scampered away. Did he realise just how lucky he was, to be able to look out and call this land his own? Four weeks ago, early yesterday even, she would have said no, without compunction. But things had changed; the ground she had thought she was so sure of had shifted a little. Yesterday evening, just before she'd bolted to the safety of her bedroom, he really had seemed different, more. . .relaxed, human. Had she imagined it?

'You're up early.'

So was he. She watched as he crossed the meadow and felt the familiar jolt in the pit of her stomach as he came near. Old, old jeans, worn-out shirt; how did he still manage to look so devastating?

'Did you sleep well?'

Robyn nodded stiffly and moved forwards, aware of his arm brushing hers as he fell into step beside her. 'As well as could be expected.'

'In the circumstances, you mean?' he enquired.

'Yes.' Robyn repeated. 'In the circumstances.'

Silence. They walked, looking, listening, enjoying the peace. Robyn waited for him to break the spell of this wonderful, strangely companionable silence. Surely he would. Everyone did eventually.

They had reached the beginning of the wood and still neither had spoken. The tangled undergrowth prevented, for the moment, exploration. Robyn paused and looked upwards into the canopy of leaves, watched the way the sunlight filtered through.

'You're so lucky,' she murmured at last. 'This is truly wonderful.'

He breathed in, gazing around slowly, eyes drinking in the beauty, and let out a sigh that was pure contentment. 'Yes. It is. I've waited a long while for this.'

She watched his expression, saw a deep abiding satisfaction. He really did love this land.

'It must have cost an awful lot, all this,' she murmured, looking around across the large expanse of land, the huge, dominating barn. 'This is a very desirable area, isn't it? Royalty all around the county. Nice if you can afford it.' She knew she had said the wrong thing the minute the words had left her mouth. Her last comment had sounded flippant, a little bitter, as if she begrudged the fact that he could afford all this, when in reality she had just said the first thing that had come into her head because he was close and because she had felt his love of the land and in doing so had glimpsed a part of him that was unknown, disturbing to her.

He gave a sharp, familiar look and she knew where she was once again. 'That's neither here nor there,' he retorted roughly. 'I chose this place because of its beauty, not because of surface values like who my neighbours are. And yes, Robyn, I can very well afford it, and more besides, but I've worked damned hard for all that I've achieved, so you can stop spoiling things with comments like that!'

'OK! Don't get so uptight!' Robyn replied hurriedly. 'I was only making conversation. There's no need to snap my head off this early in the morning. It was just an observation. What money you may possess doesn't interest me in the slightest!'

'No?' he queried with raised brows.

'No,' Robyn replied honestly. 'I'm quite happy with my clapped-out old jeep and an offer of work every now and then.' She caught his eye and found herself smiling up at him. 'And perhaps an occasional meal or two, if I can stretch to it.'

'Are you trying to elicit some sympathy?' he enquired, smiling with quite amazing effect, so that Robyn felt her heart leap a mile. 'And from me?'

'Do I look that stupid?' Robyn replied drily, luxuriating in the sudden unexpected lightness between them. 'I'm just telling you how it is for a struggling garden designer, that's all.'

'Yesterday you told me you were a successful businesswoman,' he murmured, with mock seriousness. 'What's happened?'

'And you believed me?' she asked, shaking her head.

'Pretty stupid of me, I suppose,' he replied, 'but then I always was a sucker for a sob story.'

'You?' Robyn laughed. 'Give me a break! I'm not that gullible.'

'Ah, but it seems I was.' He bent down then, plucking something from the grass, then holding it out to her with a grave smile. 'My commiserations,' he said gravely. 'You obviously have it very hard. Here—for you.'

It was a daisy. White and pink, small and perfectly formed, common perhaps, but none the less beautiful for that. She took it, fingers trembling as they grasped the fragile stem and felt the warmth of his touch. 'Thank you,' she murmured softly, gazing into his face.

There was silence, but not like before. He felt it, surely, the electricity, the tension? She watched as his eyes fell to her mouth and knew what could so easily come next.

The taste of his mouth on hers had haunted her last night in bed; the memory of that all too brief but heart-stopping kiss at the fountain all those weeks ago still burned into her, reminding, taunting her.

He was standing close, holding her breathless with his gaze, every inch of him exuding male sexuality. If he kisses me again, she thought, I'm lost. So Robyn dragged her eyes away, broke the moment with deliberate determination; her resolutions, made as she'd lain in bed last night, would not be broken so early, so easily. He would not do this to her. 'I think I'll go back now,' she muttered abruptly. 'I can't think or work properly on an empty stomach.'

His lips curved into a knowing smile, his eyes crinkling with private amusement, and Robyn felt the surge of irritation grow within her again.

'Yes, of course, if that's what you want,' he drawled lazily.

'I think we should talk,' she said, after they'd skirted the edge of the wood, after she'd found her composure again, 'about your ideas, about how you see all of this.'

He paused and turned and she watched him surveying his land, strong, sure male potency exuding from every inch of his rugged frame. 'I see,' he said after a moment's pause, 'order and elegance, bright colour, restraint, a conquering and a moulding of the less desirable aspects of nature. That tree there, for example——' He pointed and she looked across to a singularly impressive specimen of holly. 'That will have to go.'

Robyn listened, stared, digesting all that he had said and then looked back at the magnificent sixty-foot holly tree. 'But it's beautiful!' she said, after a moment. 'A little neglected perhaps, but that can be fixed. Don't you realise it's taken at least a hundred years for that to grow? You can't just cut it down because it looks untidy!'

Luke wasn't listening. He strode on, pausing at the bottom of the meadow, looking back up the slight incline towards the barn. 'I'll want a fountain, of course, and a gazebo over there and some ornamental beds,' he continued, 'the way the Victorians used to do, bedding plants, all neatly laid in rows.'

Robyn stared at him and began to think she was going mad. She could not really be hearing all this, could she? She had been wrong! So wrong. He was striding ahead now towards the stream. God! What grand ideas did he have for that?

'Now here,' he announced brutally, 'is the perfect place for one of those Japanese-style bridges. If we take down that tree there and this one here. . .'

Robyn forced herself to picture the scene he was unbelievably painting and shuddered. She'd die rather than let this happen! 'You cannot do this!' she cried breathlessly. 'I won't let you!'

He glanced across at her, eyebrows raised in surprise. 'What's the matter, Robyn?' he enquired evenly. 'You're looking flustered.'

'You know very well what's the matter. This land. Your ideas—they're impossible!'

'Impossible?' he considered. 'Oh, no, I don't think so. I'm prepared to spend more money if that's what you're worried about.'

'Money?' Robyn stormed, with hands on hips. 'Who said anything about money? I'm talking about the land, about destroying natural habitat, about brutalising nature. Fountains indeed! It will all be hideous, absolutely hideous! Can't you see that?'

'Is this your unusually polite way of saying you don't agree with my ideas?' he enquired drily. 'I think perhaps you've forgotten something——This *is* my land; I can do with it as I please. Besides——' his lips twitched infuriatingly '—what's the matter? I thought you liked fountains.'

'Over my dead body!' Robyn snapped.

'Or mine,' he murmured. 'You look fit to commit murder.' He folded his arms and considered her standing before him; she wasn't aware of it, but Robyn Drew looked beautiful, with her green eyes flashing fire, chin tilted in defiance, lips pursed formidably, ready for a fight. 'So, little Miss Angry,' he drawled, after a moment, 'I'm not unreasonable; tell me what you had in mind.'

Robyn took a deep breath and glared up at him. How could she honestly make this pigheaded man see sense? Was there any point in even wasting her breath trying to convince him? Yes, she thought, there is! I won't let him do this.

'The trees would stay,' she announced, knowing she was probably talking her way out of a job, 'almost all of them, and the ones that had to be taken down would be replaced with native specimens. Secondly, I'd make the land around the barn blend and unify with the surrounding area; it would merge with and reinforce the horizon beyond—harmonise rather than stick out like a sore thumb.' She glared at him defiantly. 'Which is what would happen if your hideous ideas were implemented. There would be no harsh colour, no ornamental flower-beds, no gazebo, no Japanese bridge and definitely no damn fountain.' She paused and took another deep breath. 'Details, of course, will take time and come later, but that's my general philosophy; that's what you would get if you asked me to complete this job for you.'

'Is it indeed? And that's your expert view—the opinion of a professional?' he enquired with a grim expression.

Robyn swallowed, registering the glint in his eyes, and looked defiant again. 'It is.'

'And you expect me to agree to all that? To go along and like ideas so totally opposed to my own?' His voice was scathing, the twist of his mouth as derisive as she had ever seen and then suddenly, puzzlingly, he smiled. Robyn saw it, registered, but didn't understand the wicked gleam in his eyes. 'What more can I say,' he added, 'except—it sounds fine—perhaps, although I would never commit myself at such an early stage, even perfect.'

'What?' Robyn's eyes were wide with confused surprise.

'I said it's perfect,' he repeated. 'Just as I've always visualised it. When can you get started?'

'But you said. . .back there you said. . .' she paused and looked incredulous. 'You were joking?' she asked, as the penny finally dropped. 'Stringing me along? How could you do such a thing?'

He raised his hands in an attitude of unconvincing surrender. 'Forgive me, Robyn, but it was a moment of pure impulse.' He moved towards her and stroked a light finger along the edge of her chin. 'You see, the truth is, you're so incredibly beautiful when you're angry—I couldn't resist.'

'Damn you!' Robyn glared and fought against the incredible effect that his touch produced. 'Everything's just a game, isn't it?'

Luke raised dark eyebrows. 'Tut-tut; no sense of humour, Robyn?'

Her eyes flicked to the overgrown stream beyond, the area where the water was at its deepest and murkiest. Right, she thought, why don't you see how it feels to be really wet for a change? He wouldn't have time to save himself; the splash as he entered the stream would be the most satisfying sound she would hear in a long time. 'No!' she replied. 'I haven't!' And she pushed him quickly and with all her force.

But somehow, damn him, he was too quick for her; somehow, with catlike reflexes, he had manoeuvred her around so that now he had hold of *her* arms and she felt herself falling backwards, and in a moment there she was in front of him, floundering in the stagnant, smelly water.

The shock of cold pond on her skin, the whole humiliation of standing drenched before him yet again, rendered her incapable of speech. How dared he do this to her? He had been the one meant to fall, to look ridiculous. Robyn let out a screech of frustration and stared down at her clothes. Wet again! She'd kill him!

She struggled to get out, slipping and sliding on the bank, falling, when she felt she almost had purchase, back again into the disgusting weed-ridden swamp. 'Don't bother to help me out—will you?' she yelled at him. 'Just stand there laughing; I could drown in here for all you care! Don't put yourself out, you rat!'

He gave a cheerful smile, stepping back, away from her frenzied splashing, relaxed, laughing at her again! 'Don't worry,' he replied, 'I wasn't planning on it. This is what you had in mind for me, Robyn? I'm not stupid enough to risk taking hold of your muddy paw now; you'll pull me in too!' He turned from her with a casual wave of his hand and began making his way back towards the barn. 'Don't stay in too long, Robyn,' he called over his shoulder. 'You might catch your death of cold.'

She stared after him furiously, splashing the water ineffectually in his direction, and registered anger, pure and intense, racing through every vein in her body. Anyone else, she thought fiercely, and I would be able to see the funny side, be able to have a laugh, a joke.

But not Luke Denner—he's humiliated me once too often! I've had it with him!

She furiously grasped hold of a clump of soggy weed and after more slipping and sliding finally managed to heave herself out. She stared down at the disgusting mass as it came away in her hand for a moment and then she marched after him with pursed lips and a determined gleam in her eyes.

When she was just about within striking distance, she flung the soaking bundle with all her might in his direction, shouted, 'Take that!' and then ran, not waiting to see if she had hit the target or not.

It didn't occur to her that she would get a good shot in. . .fine aim had never been one of her strong points— so when she heard him shout her name behind her, her instinct as ever was to run. He sounded angry. Had the muddy weed really hit its mark? Oh, cripes! What had she thrown it for anyway? It had seemed right in that split second; now she wished with all her heart that she hadn't done it. And where exactly did she think she was running to? I should have kept my temper, she thought frantically; I should never have tried to push him into the stream in the first place. You simply did not do that sort of thing to men like Luke Denner!

He was gaining on her, as always. What was he, she thought bitterly, an Olympic athlete? She could feel him behind now. So close. Any minute and he'd reach out a hand and grab her.

Robyn stopped dead in her tracks, hating the panic of the chase—she had run away from him before and look where that had got her!

It was a foolish thing to do, she knew that a fraction of a second too late; he cannoned into her with such force that she fell heavily to the ground.

Robyn lay still for a moment with her eyes closed, gasping for breath. She had fallen with such a thud and her shoulder ached painfully where she'd hit the ground.

'What the hell did you stop like that for?' he asked harshly. 'That was a stupid thing to do.'

Robyn struggled with her breathing a moment, hesitated and then gave a little groan. 'I think I've broken something—can you help?' Her voice was perfect, she estimated—appealing, weak, but with just the right amount of braveness to it.

'Oh, God!' He knelt beside her and she saw concern flash across his features. 'Don't try to move. Where does it hurt?'

Robyn worked at the pained expression and tried to decide what limb she should choose. 'My leg,' she moaned, after a slight pause. 'It's my leg.'

He bent over her and a little muddy water dripped from his hair. Robyn saw a strand of waterweed on his shoulder and suppressed a smile. 'Can you sit up at all?' he asked.

She shook her head and straightened her expression swiftly. 'No. I've hurt my back too—I don't think I can move.'

He swore quietly and then bent low, so that his face was directly over hers.

She took a breath. He was very close suddenly, too close. She swallowed nervously. 'W. . .what are you doing?' she asked breathlessly.

'Ssshh.' He pressed a finger gently to her lips. 'You shouldn't try to talk, not in your condition. How's your leg? Still painful? And your back? Broken, do you think? Perhaps your arm?' His hands touched each place, lingering, stroking. 'No, you mustn't try to move; it could be extremely dangerous. Perhaps I should remove some of this wet clothing, just so I can see the extent of your injuries.' He prevented her from rising, placing firm strong hands over her upper arms. 'I wouldn't be able to live with myself if I thought there might be permanent damage.'

'OK. Very funny.' Robyn swallowed apprehensively. 'The joke's over. Will you let me up now?'

'Uh-uh.' He shook his head and she felt the pressure of his hands. 'It's not going to be as easy as that,' he murmured. 'I think you deserve more than a certain amount of punishment for making me wet and nearly giving me a heart-attack—— Do you know how difficult it would have been to get an ambulance out here to you?' He cast his eyes over her in an unhurried, tantalising gaze, smiled a seductive, lazy smile that told Robyn only too well what was to come. 'So, let me see now. What punishment, do you think, would be fair in the circumstances?'

'None!' Robyn spat. 'Stop it, Luke! Let me up!'

'Oh, come on, Robyn, you know me well enough by now. You wouldn't honestly expect me to let you get away with that sort of behaviour, would you?' His lips curved. 'No, of course you wouldn't. I almost feel it's my duty to show you the error of your ways. In fact how am I to know you didn't do all this just so we could be in this very position now?'

'Don't flatter yourself!' Robyn snapped. 'I wouldn't demean myself or give your ego the satisfaction!'

'No?' He gave a slow, lazy smile.

'Don't you dare!' Robyn whispered fiercely.

'Dare?' he repeated. 'You're daring me?' His mouth curved formidably.

'I'm doing no such thing!' Robyn yelled, struggling ineffectually against his hold. 'Now let me up!'

'I will,' he drawled, 'when I'm ready. Don't worry, Robyn; punishment, of a certain kind, meted out in a special way, can be quite enjoyable; I promise it won't be painful.' He cast his eyes unhurriedly over her face. 'Now what would be appropriate in the circumstances? This perhaps?' His mouth was close—oh, God, so close!—almost on hers, almost caressing the softness of her lips, tantalising, tormenting, deliberately prolonging the indescribable ecstasy of desire. 'Shall I kiss you, Robyn?' he murmured huskily, breathing the words against her lips. 'Shall I? We did it once before; do you remember?' His mouth played on her face, brushing her throat, her eyes, moving over her skin like fire, back to her mouth again. She felt the tip of his tongue running along her pliant lips, the faintest touch, and yet immediately her body yearned to respond. She felt the strength of his body pressing against her own, turning her insides to a quivering mass. She couldn't breathe. He was so close, she couldn't think, she certainly couldn't speak, explain that nothing mattered except the longing, the sudden urgency, the need to feel his mouth on hers. She craved it; she wanted to taste him and touch him so much. . .

He kept her waiting, pushing her desire to the limits, enjoying the torment, the agony that was surely written all over her face.

And then he lifted his head, carefully, slowly.

There was to be a reprieve. Robyn let out a long, quivering breath and felt the treacherous ache in her body.

No punishment.

He was a bastard! A bastard to do this to her. She saw his mouth, the mouth that had so nearly covered hers, curve into a provocative smile. 'Punishment enough, I think,' he said softly, as his hands traced a deliberately sensuous path over the clinging wetness of her shirt and came to rest for the briefest of moments on the raised outline of her breasts. 'Shall we have some breakfast now?'

He rose, allowing Robyn to scramble to her feet. She glared up furiously into his self-satisfied face. 'Go to hell!' she snapped and watched as he laughed and turned then, and strode back towards the barn, whistling cheerfully beneath his breath.

Robyn wandered outside, alone with her thoughts and her anger for another hour, until hunger and a curious desire to see Luke again drove her back indoors.

He was in the kitchen, seated at the table with her holdall open beside him and the contents sprawled around. 'What do you think you're doing?' she asked. 'Those are my things.'

He glanced up, patently unperturbed by the ice in her voice, took a mouthful of coffee, and looked back down again at the book he was studying. 'Come over here. There's a picture that sums up perfectly how I want the woodland to look.'

She hesitated, furious with his calmness. Good God! How cold and calculated he was. He had turned her body to fire with a few practised touches out there and now he expected her to forget all that had happened, stand beside him and discuss the garden as if nothing in the world had just occurred.

'I don't want to see it!' she hissed. 'What's the point? I'm leaving as soon as I've had something to eat.' She went over to the hob and slammed the frying-pan on to the heat. 'I presume I'm allowed breakfast, some of this bacon and egg?' He didn't reply. So Robyn slapped several rashers into the pan and began buttering bread with a vicious sweep of the knife.

'Temper, temper!' he murmured.

She rounded on him, knife in one hand. 'Don't you "temper, temper" me!' she flashed. 'You're despicable! Childish!'

He raised cool eyebrows. 'Childish?' he retorted. 'That's pretty rich coming from someone who tried to drown her employer and then pretended she'd broken every limb in her body!'

'Don't exaggerate.' She threw him a scathing look. 'It was a trickle of a stream and I did not say I'd broken every bone, just hurt my leg. Look at the state of me now!'

'You deserved it. That temper of yours needs keeping in check. You're just mad now because I turned the tables on you.'

'I'm mad because you play juvenile pranks, telling me all those lies, letting me believe all that rubbish!'

'It was a little bit of harmless fun, that's all,' he remarked mildly. 'Nothing to get so uptight about. Some women would have taken it in good humour.'

'Well, I am not some women,' Robyn retorted. 'And besides it was a shock to the system—I really believed you capable of all those awful ideas!'

'You did? Well, thanks for that,' he murmured drily. 'And there was I imagining that underneath that hostile exterior there was a girl who really held me in high esteem.'

'Huh!' Robyn's look left him in no doubt. 'You must be joking!'

'Possibly,' he replied, 'I am. Although from our experience of just a while ago I would say that, undoubtedly, beneath that frigid exterior there lurks an inferno of quite gigantic proportions.' His lips twisted into a provocative smile. 'You had the hots for me, Robyn; why don't you just come right out and admit it?'

Robyn felt the crimson heat flood her face. 'Why, you egotistical, arrogant, big-headed. . .' She had turned the hob on too high and the bacon had begun to burn. Robyn swore and flung herself at the stove, trying to scrape what was left of the bacon away from the bottom of the pan. 'Now look what you've made me do!' she screeched. 'My breakfast is ruined!' He laughed then, at her flustered madness, and she felt like throwing the whole lot over him. 'Right! That's it!' She left the stove, grabbed her holdall and began packing everything back into it. 'I'm leaving right now! If I stay in this house with you for another minute I'm going to go quite mad.' She glared across at him. 'So don't try to stop me.'

She saw Luke's jaw tighten and a cool glint remove the sparkle that had been there before. 'I wouldn't dream of it,' he said tersely. 'If you want to leave, go right ahead, walk as far as you like. It's a futile gesture, of course, because there's nowhere for you to go.' He shrugged. 'But, if you feel the need to walk for miles in what is soon going to be very hot sun without any idea of your destination ——' he threw her a dismissive look '—well, then, that's up to you.'

Robyn glared again and caught her breath in frustration. 'I could hitch-hike,' she retorted. 'Once I got on to a main road I wouldn't have any trouble getting a lift.'

'Like hell!' he rasped. 'If that's what you have in mind then you're staying right here! You know as well as I do how dangerous it is for a woman alone on the roads— any pervert could pick you up!'

Robyn had no intention of hitch-hiking. She had never done it in her life before and she wasn't about to start now, but he didn't know that, and as the mention of getting a lift had finally wiped that superior smile from his face she felt more than inclined to pursue it. 'Will you stop telling me what I can and cannot do?' Robyn flashed. 'I'm a grown woman. I am perfectly entitled to make my own decisions and that means that I'll damn well hitch-hike if I want to!'

'No, you won't,' he repeated tightly, 'not while I'm around.' He rose from the table then, pushing a chair roughly out of his way, and Robyn flinched at the severity of his expression. 'Right,' he snapped, standing directly in front of her. 'I think it's time we got a few things clear. You are going nowhere. You are here to work. You will work. Your one wish is to complete this job to the best of your ability—and whatever that may be,' he added drily, 'you will do so. What you are not at liberty to do and what you *will not* do is storm around, losing your temper in my home. I am, for the moment, your employer, and you've accepted this job.'

'I can change my mind!' she snapped. 'You can't force me to work for you. You can't keep me here against my will!'

'Can't I?' he replied. 'Just try walking out of that door with the intention of hitch-hiking and see where it gets you!'

Robyn glanced to where he pointed and then looked up at him and folded her arms. 'I wasn't going to hitch,' she retorted. 'I just said that to make you mad.'

'Well, it worked!' he rasped, moving a step closer. 'You've got what you wanted.'

'What I want is to get out of here!' Robyn retorted. 'Remember?'

'So you want to back out?' he sneered. 'Realised it's just too difficult, have you?'

'No!' Robyn insisted. 'Not at all. I just don't happen to like working for a male chauvinistic pig like you, that's all!'

'How convenient and extremely predictable that excuse is!' he drawled. 'Do you really expect me to believe that?'

'I don't give a damn what you believe!' Robyn stormed. 'I know what I'm capable of; I know I could design this garden standing on my head if need be.'

'Suburban estates and business parks are not this garden! Oh, yes,' he added when Robyn looked up at him in surprise, 'I did a little research on you before inviting you to tender for this job—I at least go about things in a methodical and planned way. This sort of thing is out of your league; you're just too stubborn and embarrassed to admit as much to me, that's all.'

'That's not true,' she hissed furiously, 'and you know it!'

'Do I?' he queried lazily. 'You might believe you can achieve something with those acres of rough pasture and that extremely overgrown wood; I am, as yet, unconvinced.' He stepped back and folded his arms, casually surveying her dishevelled and extremely grubby figure.

Robyn tried not to care, tried not to feel a million times worse just from seeing the clearly disdainful expression, but it was impossible. With one simple look Luke Denner could make her feel completely and utterly inferior. 'So what's it to be?' he asked in clipped tones that held more than a hint of impatience. 'Earlier you agreed to produce a design. Are you standing by that, or backing out?'

CHAPTER SIX

BACKING out? Robyn thought. Letting Luke win? Her response was instantaneous. Oh, no! Not when he had stooped so low, exploited the fact that she was a woman, used his own sexual ego to ridicule her and dominate. She'd be damned if she'd let him think he could get away with that!

She raised her head and threw him a cold look. 'I'll be staying,' she announced. 'Anger, just for a moment, clouded my professional judgement. Apart from anything else, this project is worth a great deal financially and I'd be a fool to myself if I forfeited it just because the client is an obnoxious, egotistical swine. Backing out isn't my style.'

'So does this mean you're going to keep a hold of that temper,' he enquired infuriatingly, giving her an arrogant stare, 'and start acting like a professional? Well?' he insisted, when Robyn only glared up at him. 'Am I going to get a reply?'

She compressed her lips into a hard line. She could think of hundreds, no, thousands of replies just at this moment and each one had innumerable abusive words peppered throughout. She forced herself to meet his gaze, and ran a shaky hand through her curls, fighting hard to control her temper. 'I get mad because you provoke me,' she muttered, through clenched teeth, 'Leave me alone and you'll find I can contain my temper quite easily.'

'Like hell!' He laughed suddenly and all the tight irritation in his face melted away, so that, as usual, Robyn felt confused and foolish because being angry with him was so difficult and pointless when his mouth curved into that wonderful smile and his eyes sparkled so. 'OK, you may take it you are suitably reprimanded,' he drawled infuriatingly. 'Now I've got work to do, and so, I should imagine, have you.'

She gathered information all morning; taking accurate measurements and soil tests, pin-pointing particular features or specimens on her plan, even photographs to remind her for when she got back to her drawing-board and began designing.

It was hot work. By early afternoon she had had enough and returned to the barn, desperate for the cool interior and something to eat. She longed for some proper clothes too—having to wear one of his large baggy T-shirts was doing nothing for her self-image.

She wandered into the kitchen, pleased with her work, relieved too that Luke didn't seem to be about. In fact, she thought as she splashed cold water on to her hot face, she hadn't seen him all morning—perhaps he'd taken himself off for a walk.

She dried her face and hands and then opened the fridge door. She hadn't been able to stomach a great deal at breakfast, not after everything that had happened; now she was starving.

Inside the fridge, propped between two cans of lager, was a note, behind which was an appetising plateful of sandwiches. Robyn read, 'A PEACE OFFERING. Luke.'

The sandwiches looked good—succulent fillings and soft fresh bread. Robyn picked up the piece of paper and tried hard not to believe he had made an effort. So he wanted peace. Well, that was novel. But why? So far she had gained the distinct impression that being angry and obnoxious with her suited him just fine—he positively revelled in deriding her at every opportunity. So what was with the sudden change? And besides, she thought irritably, did she even want to be on speaking terms with him after the way he had treated her? When they were mad with one another, at least she knew where she was, how she should behave. . .

She heard his footsteps in the hall and her jumbled thoughts halted in their tracks as he entered, hands thrust casually into the pockets of his denims.

Robyn watched him cautiously as he bent to the fridge. He picked up a can, ripped the ring-pull and held it out to her. 'You look hot,' he murmured. 'Care for a drink?'

She did care, very much. Her mouth was as dry as a bone, but she resisted, ignoring the can he proffered, and stared resolutely up at him. 'A truce?' she enquired stony-faced. 'Is it possible?'

'We could work at it,' he replied evenly. 'We are going to spend a few more hours in one another's company; it would make life easier.'

'Be civil, do you mean?' she asked.

His lips twisted into a thrilling smile at her tone of scepticism and Robyn felt her heart flip over once again. 'You're right,' he drawled, 'Forget it. 'It does seem rather an absurd idea, after all "civil" covers the middle ground, and somehow I don't think that area exists for us.' He threw her a direct, heart-stopping look. 'All or nothing's more our style, wouldn't you say, Robyn?'

She was silent for a moment, helplessly imagining what the 'all' he spoke of would be like; passionate possession of the most delicious kind invaded her thoughts, an ecstasy so far only dreamed of—fierce and completely fulfilling. . . Robyn swallowed and blushed and thanked God he couldn't read her mind. '"Civil" seems sensible,' she said after a moment, in as firm a voice as possible, 'I think I can manage that.'

'Good,' he replied, ripping open another can. 'Let's drink to it, then.' He held up the can of lager. 'Our shaky truce,' he announced with mock ceremony. 'Long may it hold.'

It was early evening when the telephone rang. Robyn had somehow got into the position of cooking dinner, not wanting to admit that the simple process of preparing and cooking a meal for Luke filled her with dread. They were together in the kitchen deciding what to have.

It was a short call. He replaced the receiver and said, 'You'd better do enough for four.'

She looked up at the sound of his voice; he didn't sound particularly pleased. 'Why?' she enquired, as she began to peel and chop onions. 'Are you feeling that hungry?'

'No,' Luke replied. 'That was my business partner Paul; he and his wife are here—or rather they're almost here—they're stuck on the wrong side of your jeep. I'm going to go and pick them up now.'

'You were expecting them?'

He shook his head. 'Not at all, but it seems they were in the area, so they decided to drop in.'

Robyn glanced down at the chopping-board; cooking for him would be bad enough, but others? 'Will spaghetti bolognese be all right?' she asked uncertainly. 'We did decide on pasta.'

He picked up his keys and shrugged. 'Fine. Hey, don't look so worried, Robyn. If they will insist on arriving unexpectedly, they'll have to like it or lump it, won't they? I'll be back in a minute.'

It's not only the menu that worries me, Robyn thought despondently, as she heard the Range Rover start up; what about the way I look and feel? She was a wreck and had planned to go and do something about it once dinner had been prepared, but now that would have to go by the board—there would be no time—and, besides, she could hardly appear to Luke's business partner and his wife in one of Luke's towelling robes, could she? Goodness knew what they'd think!

They thought it all anyway.

Robyn could tell the minute she met their curious glances. I might as well have had that shower, she thought drily; at least I would have felt a hundred times more human.

Melissa was a bitch. Robyn could sense it; the hostile vibes that emanated from her as soon as she saw Robyn were almost tangible, and the frosty smile and ice-cold gaze on introduction merely confirmed what Robyn already knew. She got the distinct impression that Melissa wasn't best pleased to find that Luke had company.

Her husband seemed better. A nice firm handshake on introduction, pleasant, relaxed smile with no hint of hostility, just the expected male gleam of curiosity.

Luke poured drinks and Robyn accepted hers gratefully. She needed something. The humiliation of standing beside a woman who smelt, dressed and looked absolutely wonderful was doing little for her ego. I'm not even clean! she thought desperately.

They were chatting; Robyn returned to the hob and nervously added the rest of the ingredients to the sauce.

'Known Luke long, have you?' Melissa asked, casting interested eyes over Robyn's dishevelled figure.

Robyn wasted her most pleasant smile. 'No, not at all,' she replied.

Melissa was hoping for a little more information, Robyn could see that. 'Oh, so you're just some sort of brief acquaintance, then?' she murmured, adding softly as she prepared to sip her drink, so that only Robyn could catch her words, 'Luke tends to have those from time to time. It's his one weakness, I suppose.'

Her implication was plain. Robyn whipped the sauce around viciously in the pan and was frantically trying to think up some caustic reply, when Luke interjected smoothly, 'Robyn's not an acquaintance, Melissa.' There was a slight edge to his voice. 'She's here for a purpose,' he added.

Robyn's heart sank. The unfortunate phrasing of his sentence hardly made things sound any better. She threw him a suspicious look. Was he deliberately trying to make her feel even more humiliated?

Melissa's arched eyebrows rose into her hairline and her mouth twitched suggestively. Robyn glanced across at her and fought the impulse to pour the bolognese sauce right over the expensively coiffured hairstyle.

'I'm a garden designer,' she announced quietly, staring down at the hob, 'that's what Luke meant.'

'Indeed?' Melissa replied. 'So the vehicle that's blocking the track belongs to you?'

'Yes,' Robyn replied sweetly. 'How clever of you to work it out. It broke down.'

'I'm not surprised,' Melissa remarked. 'It seems pretty dilapidated.' She turned to her husband. 'We thought someone had abandoned it there, didn't we, darling? Must be hard times for garden designers,' Melissa added acidly, 'if the state of your vehicle is anything to go by—obviously not much work around.'

'There's enough,' Robyn replied shortly. 'I get by.'

'But only just,' Melissa insisted, with a particularly irritating catlike smile. She looked Robyn up and down once more. 'Forgive my asking,' she added, 'But aren't you wearing rather impractical gear for grubbing around in the earth or whatever it is you do?'

'No, not at all,' Robyn murmured through clenched teeth, 'because, you see, I don't grub around as you so delicately put it—I design.' She managed a smile. 'There is a difference.'

'Robyn has a thing about water, Melissa,' Luke explained. 'She fell into the stream. Actually,' he added, 'Robyn loves water; she was particularly fond of the fountain at your place.' He turned to her, eyes gleaming with amusement. 'Weren't you, Robyn?'

'Oh, you've seen our little abode, then?' Paul said cheerfully. 'You were at the party.'

Robyn nodded and tried to decide who she'd throttle first—Luke or dear Melissa.

'Oh, I see. So is that where Luke first spotted your. . .talent?' Melissa enquired with deliberate emphasis.

Robyn gave her a frosty look. 'Not exactly,' she replied. 'Actually,' she added swiftly, 'I got very drunk that night, fell in your fountain, and Luke gallantly fished me out. He's very strong, isn't he? Acres of rippling muscle. But then,' she mumured sweetly, 'I'm sure you've noticed that, Melissa.' Melissa's mouth sagged open just a little and Robyn's smile was pure satisfaction. 'Of course, it was so late,' she continued with an innocent expression, 'I had to stay the night.' She turned to Luke and raised an enquiring brow. 'You woke me at—what time was it? Seven? Seven-thirty?'

'Nearer seven, I believe.' Luke's voice was dry. 'Robyn, the sauce is burning. I think you'd better see to it. We do want a meal that is at least edible.'

Robyn went over to the stove and gave the mixture a savage, scowling stir. 'It needs a few more minutes, so I think I'll go upstairs,' she announced, throwing Luke a cool glance. 'Dinner will be ready in about half an hour if anyone is interested.'

* * *

The spaghetti bolognese was acceptable; Robyn had tried her best and it wasn't a disaster. What more could she hope for? I could hope that they'll leave before dessert, she thought bitterly, as Melissa's affected laugh rang in her ear for the fourth time. Any more of her little digs at me and her sickening smiles of lust at Luke and I shall vomit. It's quite pathetic, Robyn thought, demeaning, the way she hangs on to his every word, flirts so outrageously with him. He's not taking any more notice of her than he is of me. We might as well both be invisible, she told herself with irritation, conveniently forgetting Luke's earlier attempts to draw her into the conversation.

She listened for the first time in ages, pouring herself another glass of wine, knowing she was drinking a little too much, but doing it out of a desire to annoy Luke. The conversation had shifted; now they were talking business.

'You clinched the deal with Philip, then?' Paul was saying. 'That was good going, Luke. Filming can start on schedule, thank God! For a while there I thought we were going to be up the creek without a paddle.'

Robyn took a sip and wished she had been listening from the beginning. Filming? Wasn't that what he'd said?

Melissa dabbed daintily at her mouth. 'How's casting going, Luke? Have you got who you want?'

Luke nodded. 'Yes,' he replied, 'I confirmed yesterday evening. 'We're going to start shooting at the end of the month.'

'Films?' Robyn demanded, slapping down her wine glass on to the table. 'You're in the film business?'

The three of them turned and looked at her. Her voice, she realised, had been a little strident. Luke answered for them all. 'Yes, that's right,' he said. 'Are you interested in film-making, Robyn?'

Robyn felt the blood drain from her face, she could hear the sudden hammering of her heart. 'I. . . I didn't realise,' she mumbled. 'Why didn't you tell me?'

Luke shrugged nonchalantly. 'I don't know; the subject never came up, I suppose. Does it matter, then?' he challenged.

'No. No, of course not.' Robyn stared down at her plate, managed a mouthful of bolognese. She had been wrong before—it tasted awful.

'We all make our living from the film industry in one area or another,' he continued. 'Paul and I have a production company—I direct as well—and Melissa here is an actress——'

'Oh, surely you've heard of Luke!' Melissa cut in. 'You must have! He's such a respected figure in the film industry!' She rattled off the names of films he had apparently directed, looking overtly scornful at Robyn's ignorance.

Robyn shook her head. 'I don't go to the cinema very often,' she murmured. 'I haven't the time.'

'Are you OK?' Luke's eyes were scanning her face. 'You look a little pale suddenly. Don't you feel well?'

Robyn twisted her gaze away. 'No. Yes! I mean I'm all right! Don't fuss. I'm fine,' she snapped.

There was a moment's pause; they were digesting her rudeness, she could see that. Paul shifted uncomfortably in his seat.

Luke rose. 'So, time for dessert, I think. Robyn, perhaps you'd like to help me clear the dishes,' he instructed, giving her a warning glance. 'Like now?' he added pointedly when Robyn stared vacantly into space and made no move.

She got up, grabbing her own plate and that of Melissa, not noticing as the spaghetti slid dangerously near to the edge of the plate. 'Watch out!' Melissa backed off in alarm. 'For goodness' sake!' she added in high-pitch tones. 'This dress cost an absolute fortune. Can't you watch what you're doing? Look, there's a splash of sauce on my sleeve.'

Be thankful I didn't tip it over your head! Robyn muttered silently. She grabbed a serviette and aloud said sweetly, 'Here, let me scrub at it for you. I'll soon get it out.'

'No, no! It's all right.' Melissa backed away some

more. 'You'll just make it worse. I'll go upstairs and see to it.'

Luke followed Robyn into the kitchen. 'Don't you dare!' he warned, once they had set the plates onto the draining-board. 'I'm not having you acting like a kid this evening. You're drinking too much,' he added bluntly. 'Lay off the wine and start being civil. It won't kill you.'

'How do you know?' Robyn argued. 'If I have to listen to that dreadful Melissa for another hour, I might just die of boredom. She's. . .she's——'

'I know what she is,' Luke interrupted coldly. 'I don't need you to tell me, but Paul's a partner and a good friend. I'd like it to stay that way, do you hear? Now, there's some mousse in the fridge,' he said roughly. 'Get it out and I'll take the dishes through. ' He turned at the kitchen door. 'And remember I mean what I say, Robyn—no more stupidity or I might not be responsible for my actions.'

The conversation was picked up from somewhere off the floor once dessert arrived and the three of them were talking again. On home ground. Films past, projects to come, anecdotes about people she'd never heard of—faceless names from a profession that small-time landscape designer Robyn Drew knew little about—shooting schedules and post-production, contracts and distribution deals.

Robyn listened helplessly as they talked around and about her and remembered. For this world they inhabited, this world they talked so animatedly about, had been the world her brother had loved, the world where he had lived.. . .and died. Would his story perhaps, in the months ahead, become a dinner table topic? she wondered.

'Of course, it's not all a bed of roses,' she could hear someone say. 'Did you hear about that actor—can't remember his name, talented, though, good prospects—who had that terrible accident? Plunged to his death while filming on location in France. High-spirited sort of chap by all accounts. . .such a waste——!'

'My brother was an actor,' she said suddenly, cutting through another of Melissa's boring dialogues.

They all glanced at her. 'Really?' Luke murmured politely. 'What sort of work?'

Robyn blanched. Why had she blurted that out, for heaven's sake? She glanced away uncomfortably, staring down at her plate, fiddling with her spoon, wishing she hadn't said anything. 'Oh—um—all sorts,' she muttered after a pause. 'Anything he could get.'

'But he's not in acting now?' Melissa enquired.

'No,' Robyn replied. 'But he was good,' she added with a sort of pathetic defiance. 'Very good.'

'Oh, well, some make it to the big time, others don't,' Melissa remarked smugly. 'Not everyone has the dedication, or the talent, of course, to reach great heights. Our profession is a particularly competitive one, isn't it, Luke?' Melissa placed a proprietorial hand on his arm. 'Although you and I have done pretty well, haven't we, darling?'

'Well, bully for you!' Robyn remarked tautly, glaring across the table. 'Although I think your idea of success, Melissa, is quite obviously very different from mine.'

'And just what do you mean by that?' Melissa retorted archly. 'I'm a well-known actress.'

Robyn threw her napkin on to her plate, scraped back her chair and stood up. 'You're in that early-evening soap opera, aren't you—the one set in a hospital?' Robyn asked.

Melissa's nod showed her satisfaction.

'And you class that as success?' Robyn made her voice sound particularly scathing. 'I'd rather grub around in the earth any day!' She turned to Luke. 'Thank you so much,' she said sarcastically, 'for allowing me to eat with such revered company, but I'm tired now. I've had enough. I'm going to bed.'

Luke took the visitors back to their car some time after eleven. Robyn rested her head on her arms on the sill of the open window and listened as he climbed the spiral staircase.

He would be angry with her, of course. Another completely juvenile performance, as far as he was concerned. But what should she care? That was the least of her troubles.

There was a knock on the door and she stiffened, her breath stilling in the throat.

'Can I come in?'

She didn't reply.

'Robyn, answer me! I know you're not asleep.'

How did he know? she wondered angrily. How could he possibly tell?

Leave me alone! she thought. Just leave me alone.

He gave her two seconds and then the door opened wide and he stood, large and menacing, in the moonlit room. He flicked on the light.

'Don't!' Her voice was sharp. 'I like it dark.'

'Tough!' he barked.

There was silence. 'Well, say it, then!' Robyn demanded fiercely. 'Start lecturing me on bad manners. That's what you're here for, isn't it?'

'I wouldn't waste my time, Robyn,' he snapped sarcastically. 'You know enough about bad manners to last a lifetime! That was quite a performance you gave this evening.'

'So?' Robyn muttered. 'I didn't ask to sit down to dinner with them, I didn't ask to be ridiculed and insulted by dear, delightful Melissa!'

'So you were rude! How original of you!' he sneered.

'She started it—all her implications, her little digs at me. Why should I take that from someone like her?' Robyn turned back to the window, longed to be away, among those hills silhouetted in the moonlight.

'She can be catty, I know that, but you made things far worse than they needed be,' Luke retorted. 'You were determined to spoil the evening from the very first.'

'Me? That's downright unfair!' Robyn shot back. 'How can you stand there and say that?'

'Quite easily—I just open my mouth and the words fall out!' he growled. 'Very similar, in fact, to the way yours did earlier this evening—Melissa did not take kindly to your remarks about her.'

'Good! She deserved it,' Robyn retorted. 'My brother was a fine actor and I won't let her——' she turned and glared at him '—or anyone else, for that matter, imply otherwise.'

'Leave me out of this!' he replied coolly. 'I didn't say a thing!'

'No, but you undoubtedly thought much the same,' she replied bitterly. 'After all, how could I ever possess a brother who was remotely talented? Juvenile Robyn Drew? No! Of course not! Too ridiculous for words!'

She was trembling with anger, her pulse beating wildly in her chest. She was furious—with Melissa, with herself, with him. 'This is all a complete waste of time, isn't it?' she added. 'Me struggling to prove a point when all the time you've decided, made up your mind.'

He stood and looked at her for a moment, hands on hips, jaw set. 'What are you referring to now—the garden?'

'Yes! No! Oh, I don't know! The garden, me! You've made up your mind and that's going to be it. Why you ever asked me down in the first place is still a mystery to me. Oh, but of course,' she added harshly, 'I forgot; that was just a whim on your part, wasn't it? A little experiment!'

His eyes hadn't left her face; they were thoughtful, searching. Robyn took ragged breaths and then tore her eyes away.

'What the hell is all this? There's something else, isn't there, Robyn?' he said tersely. 'You're really upset— why? I can't believe it's because some silly woman like Melissa had a go at you.'

She hesitated, thought of Mark, her grief for him, for the way he had wasted his life, and then looked at Luke. Wasn't he the reason for her anger? This man who somehow made her feel so good and yet so bad, all at the same time. What am I doing here? She thought. Why am I putting myself through all this?

'Will you please speak to me, for God's sake? Robyn, look, forget this evening, forget Melissa. Just give me some sort of explanation. Believe it or not but I would like to understand.'

How odd, she thought. He's trying hard to be patient,

really trying—it was the last thing she had expected, such a shame she couldn't reward him.

'I just didn't like them,' she murmured. 'You and your patronising friends—huh!' It was the truth, just not the right answer to his particular question.

She heard the sharp intake of breath; what little patience he possessed had clearly vanished with her last smart remark. 'Funnily enough, they didn't think a great deal of you!' he snarled.

'As if I care!' Robyn retorted.

'This is pointless, isn't it?' he snapped. 'Absolutely pointless! You are the most stubborn, irritating child I have ever come across! Well, in the morning, when you've got over your fit of pique, about I don't know what, I'll expect an apology from you. Is that damn well clear?'

CHAPTER SEVEN

LUKE slammed the door.

Robyn stared out and tried to control her trembling bottom lip. 'I will not cry!' she muttered fiercely. 'I will not!'

She sat for a long while, until her limbs became cold and stiff and her mind numb with tiredness and misery. Then she rose and went over to the bed, pulled back the covers and slipped between the cool, fresh sheets. Sleep, desperately needed, wouldn't come. Robyn lay, eyes closed, and concentrated on keeping her mind blank and her body relaxed. She felt so tired, so emotionally exhausted.

I must relax, she thought. I must.

When she could stand it no longer, she flung back the bedclothes and crossed to the washbasin in the corner of the room, splashing her face with cold water. A book perhaps; that might do the trick—she could read a while. She peered at her wristwatch and saw with surprise that it was almost one. Two hours she had lain there—two whole hours of torment.

She crept stealthily along the gallery, not daring to put on a light in case she should wake Luke, past his room, feeling carefully in the half-darkness.

When he appeared in the doorway to his bedroom, she gasped and leapt, her nerves like coiled springs, clutching at her heart.

'What are you doing?' His voice was alert, not the least bit sleepy, although clearly he had just woken.

She caught a glimpse of the ruffled bed beyond, noted his tousled hair and hastily tied robe, covering very little of his tanned torso, and wished quite desperately that they didn't hate each other.

'I. . . I couldn't sleep. I just thought I'd go down and get a book.'

'Not tired after all?' he enquired coldly.

'I. . . I was. I mean I am. But I just don't seem able to get to sleep.' Robyn's voice quivered and she could feel the tears, held back for so long, welling up inside.

She moved to go past him, but he shot out a hand and restrained her. He stared down at her for a few seconds, almost as if searching for some clue hidden in her expression. 'For God's sake, Robyn, tell me. Is there something worrying you? You don't seem yourself.'

'I'm fine!' Her voice was unnecessarily harsh, over-compensation for the misery and tension.

'You don't look fine to me,' he commented coolly, flicking a strand of hair back from her cheek. 'What is it? Don't you feel well?'

She took a deep breath, keeping her eyes from his tanned face. 'I'm all right,' she repeated, as if convincing not only him, but herself too. 'I am. I can sort things out for myself.'

'So there is something, then,' he returned, 'something that's on your mind? Is it the garden? Are you worrying about that?' When she didn't reply he added, 'Look, things have a knack of seeming unsolvable in the small hours—out of proportion; it is a large job, I realise that, but you're probably worrying about nothing.'

Robyn gave a short, derisive laugh and shook her head. 'The garden?' she asked with angry incredulity. 'You think I'd lie awake worrying about something as trivial as that?'

'OK, OK,' he replied irritably. 'Calm down! So it's not the garden! But there is something, isn't there?' he persisted grimly. 'You are lying awake worrying about something. . .some difficulty?'

Robyn's gaze fell to the floor. 'It doesn't matter,' she mumbled. 'My life, like everyone else's, is full of problems, difficulties, whatever you care to call them. It's something that I've got to work out by myself.'

'But there are some problems that are more difficult to solve than others, aren't there?' he insisted.

She glared up, aware of the slight change in his tone, and saw that his eyes were scouring hers with a strange kind of intensity. She hesitated; his gaze was so power-ful, so strong. She fought against the sudden unexplainable impulse to tell him everything, to lighten the heavy burden of grieving alone. The words were there, waiting to spill out. If only she could, if only he would understand. . .

'Are you pregnant, Robyn?' he asked evenly. 'Is that what all this is about?'

It was as if he had slapped her in the face. She stared at him in astonishment for several silent seconds, hardly able to believe her own ears.

'Pregnant.' She repeated the word softly, testing the sound of it on her lips, as if it were a word she had never heard before. If it had been suggested at any other time, by anyone else, she probably would have laughed, dismissed the suggestion, treated it with casual indifference. But not here, not now, not with this man. She lifted her head, brought her eyes around until she stared into his swarthy, angular face. 'That's what you think?' she asked calmly, quietly, knowing all the while exactly what he thought.

'It crossed my mind,' he murmured stiffly. 'Your swings of mood, your erratic behaviour. Isn't that how it affects some women?'

'Yes.' It was perfectly true; she had had a friend once who'd changed personality at the drop of a hat as soon as she had conceived. Will it happen to me, she thought, when, or if, I ever have a child? She placed a hand instinctively over her stomach and wondered how it must feel to create new life inside your body. Such a beautiful, beautiful thing. . .to have someone to care about, something that was a part of you, growing inside. . .

She placed a frantic hand across her eyes; now Mark had gone, there was no one—she was alone in the world. . . She was going to cry; if he said any more, she would.

'Does your boyfriend know?'

She pressed her lips together and looked away. God! He really did believe it! Robyn shook her head and struggled against the tears. 'I. . . I don't have a boyfriend! There's just me—just Robyn Drew,' she added with sudden harshness.

'I see.' His voice was grim.

'You think I'm a tramp, don't you, Luke? she asked suddenly. 'Oh, don't bother to reply,' she swept on bitterly. 'I can see it in your face. . .ever since that party. . .' She swallowed painfully. 'Ever since that damn party! You think you know what sort of a girl I am, the sort of life I lead, don't you?' Her voice was rising with every new syllable.

'Calm down, Robyn; getting hysterical will do no good!'

'In my condition, you mean?' Robyn snapped. 'Well, why would you care? A loose girl who sleeps around and has got herself pregnant! I shouldn't think——'

He took her by the shoulders suddenly, his expression so fierce that Robyn gasped. 'I did not say you slept around! Don't you dare put words into my mouth!'

'But you think I'm pregnant?' Robyn said dully.

'It's crossed my mind. It's a possibility, a solution, it would explain a lot of things. I thought. . .look, I didn't mean it as some sort of slur on your character—there's no crime in conceiving a child, for heavens sake!'

'Even if you don't happen to know who the father is?' Robyn enquired bitterly.

He tightened his grip and pushed her back against the door-jamb suddenly. He was close, his powerful, bare chest pressing up against the towelling of her robe; she could almost feel the anger pumping around his body. 'So tell me you're not pregnant!' he commanded. 'Tell me I've got it all wrong! Talk to me. I'll believe anything you have to say.'

'How very big of you!' she snapped. 'Am I supposed to feel honoured?'

She watched as his eyes burned into her face. 'You really do like to make things difficult, don't you?' he snarled. 'Why I'm even bothering to have a conversation with you at this unearthly hour is beyond me!'

'Well, let me go, then!' she whispered vehemently. 'Save your breath; you're hurting me!'

He held her for a moment longer, glaring down at her, crushing her with his body, his fingers. And then his hands dropped from her arms and he turned and went into his bedroom. Their eyes met for a split second, bleak green against ice-blue, and in that fleeting moment she wanted to tell him the truth, she wanted to explain, repaint the picture that had been mistakenly built up. It mattered so much suddenly. She wanted him to know about her life, about her real self.

I'm a virgin! she screamed silently.

But the door closed quietly and he left her on the dark, unfamiliar landing, crying, just like a baby.

It was a day like no other. Robyn lay on her back looking up at the cloudless sky. It was so large, she thought, covering the world in a dome of pure azure. She rolled over happily and got to her feet laughing. Something in the distance, half-hidden among the trees, caught her eye. It was a house. She ran like the wind towards it, and then somehow she was inside.

There was a party in the ballroom: sparkling chandeliers, string quartet. Now where was Mark? He had said he'd meet her here. She moved through the crowd, dodging elbows, murmuring apologies, aware of a growing panic inside. There was some danger. She had to speak to him, tell him something, warn him. What was it? She looked up. He had disappeared. Where had he gone? Why would no one tell her?

Into a different room now. High, high ceilings, like in a cathedral—dim, dusty, bare. Along corridors, endless corridors, with doors on either side. She ran, her feet echoing on the cold, hard floor. He was here somewhere. She knew it. She had to find him; if she didn't something terrible would happen.

And then a door ahead. A different door—larger, special—and she felt relief wash over her. This was it. She knew it. Mark would be in here. She opened it frantically, half wrenching the door off its hinges, and looked down, screaming as the expected room disappeared and she saw nothing except a terrifying precipice and below, lying crashed and sprawled on the rocks, Mark. His body.

No! No! He was alive! She couldn't bear it! She gave an anguished cry, calling his name. And then she felt someone holding her and she had to fight; they would throw her over too. And she didn't want to die. . .not like Mark. . .not like Mark.

'Robyn, Robyn! Stop it! Robyn, wake up! It's a dream, just a dream.'

The voice was deep, commanding. But she didn't like this voice. It had hurt her, hadn't it? She fought as hard as she could against the iron grip, the bands of steel that were restricting her, trying to push her over like Mark.

She heard the voice again, over and over, calling her name, and then gradually she realised that it didn't come from the dream and she opened her eyes, staring breathless into the darkness.

She was sitting upright in bed and he was holding her close. She could smell the freshness of his skin, feel the familiar roughness of his robe against her face.

She breathed deeply, resting her head against his shoulder, exhausted by the anguish of the dream, the battle with Luke, screwing her eyes shut against the still vivid pictures in her mind.

'Are you OK now?' His voice was strangely comforting, close and soft; she could feel the warmth of his breath against her neck. I shouldn't feel so glad that he's here, she thought; I shouldn't.

'Robyn?'

She swallowed, struggling against the tightness in her throat, the sobs that threatened to overwhelm her.

'Hey, come on! It was just a dream; everything's all right,' he murmured softly. 'You're safe.' She felt his arms tighten around her in a comforting hug and just for a few seconds she allowed herself the luxury of sinking against him, feeling the strength and the warmth of his body next to her skin. Then he loosened his hold and tilted her back, so that she could see his outline in the half-light. 'Better now?' he asked.

She swallowed, wiping ineffectually at the wetness on her cheeks. 'I need some tissues,' she whispered hoarsely.

He released her, reaching carefully over to the bedside cabinet, and pulled out a box. 'Here, let me do it.'

He stroked away her tears, gently, without any hint of awkwardness, as if, Robyn thought, it were the most natural thing in the world. Had he forgotten how they'd parted just a few hours earlier? The animosity that there was between them?

'I'll put on the light; it will make the dream seem less real.'

He clicked on the lamp and the room was filled with a soft glow. He was beside her on the bed, his robe, like before, hurriedly thrown on, every inch of him exuding male potency, large and strong and tanned and full of life. He frowned down at her as she lay back self-consciously against the pillows. 'So do you get nightmares like this often?' he asked. 'It must have been pretty bad; you were shouting and screaming the place down.' Robyn's insides clenched into a tight ball. She swallowed and looked down at the duvet, twisting its striped design unhappily between her fingers. 'Sorry,' he murmured, 'shouldn't have asked; nightmares like that are undoubtedly best forgotten.'

But it was too late; large tears rolled down her cheeks and, no matter how swiftly she swiped them away and pretended they weren't there, they just kept on coming. 'Robyn, don't cry any more; you'll make yourself ill.' His voice was strong, commanding, forcing her to listen. She felt the comfort of his hand against her hair, stroking back the curls. And then she felt him move away and she lifted her head and saw that he was going towards the door.

'W. . .where are you going?' Robyn's voice quivered.

'It's OK, I'll be back.'

She watched him through the open door, saw him click on the gallery light—tall, virile, handsome, strong. . . She closed her eyes. And he could be kind; she wasn't imagining it, was she? He had held her and comforted her, wiped away her tears without any trace of scorn or mockery, hadn't he? She glanced around the room, laying her hot flushed face against the cool pillow, listening to the bang of a cupboard door below, the chinks of crockery. The room seemed empty without him, strange and unfriendly. Robyn swallowed and took a deep breath, trying to compose herself so that when he returned she could say that it was all right, she felt fine now. He could go.

When he did return he was carrying a tray; there was a tall glass of milk, a plate of biscuits.

'Here, drink this—it will make you feel better.' He held out the glass and watched as she raised it gratefully to her lips. The cool milk tasted delicious—a steadying, soothing drink that transported Robyn back to the days when her mother had cosseted her with supper in bed as a child. She drank slowly, found she was indeed hungry and munched a little on a biscuit. She had expected him to leave her but he stayed watching her quietly, picking a biscuit off the plate himself, sharing her milk when she offered him the glass.

Robyn stifled a yawn suddenly, a reaction to so much crying, but also because sleep and exhaustion were rapidly overtaking her.

'Good. You're tired.'

He rose then as if to go but impulsively Robyn caught at the sleeve of his robe. 'Can you stay?' she whispered. 'Sit beside me on the bed, just for a little while longer, until I get to sleep?'

He hesitated, gazing down at her, and suddenly she sensed, but didn't understand, the change in him, the change in his look. 'Robyn. . .' his voice was different suddenly. 'I'm not sure if that would be a good idea——'

'Please, Luke!' Robyn interrupted swiftly, unaware of anything except her need, her longing to continue this wonderful feeling of companionship. It was something that she would never have thought possible and now that it had actually happened, now that she knew she wasn't dreaming, she wanted it to last.

'All right.' He gave her a reassuring smile. 'I'll stay just for a while longer. Lie down now.' He sat on the bed and leant back against the pillow, stretching his long legs along the edge of the bed, and Robyn relaxed next to him, laying her head down thankfully by his side.

But it wasn't the same. She couldn't sleep, she couldn't recapture the way it had been before. The time for comfort had passed, the innocent desire to be held

safe and sure within his arms was gone. She was aware
of him. Every nerve-ending signalled the excitement of
feeling his body close to hers. She couldn't breathe
without thinking about him. It was no use. Desire was
overtaking fear and sorrow.

She wanted him.

Close your eyes, she told herself. Breathe gently, don't
move. But with every moment she became more and
more aware of his touch, of the way his arm felt next to
her skin, of the strength of his body pressed against her
own.

She opened her eyes, closed them again, looked up,
tried to read his profile in the half-light. His eyes were
closed. Was he asleep?

'Robyn,' he murmured roughly, 'this just isn't going
to work. I'm going to leave you.' He opened his eyes
and gazed down at her face. 'You understand why,
don't you?'

She didn't reply. Their eyes locked. Time stood still.
She saw his gaze fall to her mouth and she looked at
him and waited, wanting him to kiss her, hardly daring
to move in case the moment, the spell should be broken.
His lips came closer, so very close, and Robyn felt the
breath still within her. She raised her face, desperate for
his touch, brushing her lips lightly against his own. And
then he gave a small moan and the last vestiges of
restraint were gone. His mouth consumed hers, plundered, ravaged. He kissed her again and again and when
her arms came up and tangled in his hair, when she
kissed him as he was kissing her, she felt his hands
search and roam, slipping inside her gown, caressing
each breast, teasing, arousing, until the nipples rose
hard and firm.

'You're beautiful, so very beautiful, Robyn,' he
groaned. 'God, how I want you.' His mouth smothered
hers again and she was aware of his taut, hard body
lying across her own pliant form, aware of the roughness
of his chest, the sculptured contours of muscle that
rippled through her fingers as they clutched and stroked
at his skin. He was every inch a man and he desired her.

Then something happened; his mouth, his hands

stopped burning their trail of delight. His body stiffened; there was a change in him, Robyn felt it, knew it and then he drew back and she saw in a fleeting moment his own look of self-disgust.

He sat up on the bed, turning away from her, running a hand through his hair. 'That shouldn't have happened,' he informed her curtly. 'I'm sorry.'

Robyn closed her eyes for a second, agonised by the simple, harsh hurt of his words, balling her fists so that her nails dug deep into her palms. Sorry—again.

He was sorry? Robyn remembered being by the fountain, all those weeks ago; he had used the very same expression then. It shouldn't have happened. Why not? she cried silently. Why ever not? I wanted it, you wanted it. How could something that felt so right make you look like this, as if you had just committed the worst crime in the world?

And then she remembered. Before, on the landing, the things he had said to her, thought of her. . .Of course; it had slipped her mind. She was pregnant.

'You'd better go,' she said flatly, pulling the gown close around her body, 'before you do or say something else that you might regret.' He looked at her and was about to say something more. 'Don't!' Robyn muttered fiercely. 'Don't say another word. Just leave me.' She stared down at the crumpled bed as the door clicked quietly behind him, and then buried her face miserably into the pillow.

When she opened her eyes again she knew it was late. She lay on her back staring up at the ceiling and her thoughts immediately flashed back to Luke and last night. How could she ever face him again? She screwed her eyes tight shut, trying to forget the images of last night. I might as well have pleaded aloud with him to make love to me, she thought, I wanted him so much!

She turned over and felt an agonising wave of humiliation sweep over her, as she remembered his expression. His body wanted me, she thought, but that was all— not his mind, certainly not his heart. Sex—it was just about sex. And when he remembered who I was, what he thought I was—well, that was it! Desire killed in two seconds flat!

She stared at the clock miserably. She had slept late; it was gone eleven. She had to get up, see about the jeep, see about getting right away from here.

By the time she had made it downstairs, she felt pretty awful—hot and aching and nauseous, with the most terrible pain hanging excruciatingly over one side of her face.

Luke was in the kitchen removing the clean dishes from the dishwasher. Robyn watched him for a moment unseen, clutching at the door, forcing herself to feel all right. Then he turned and saw her and she blushed and felt foolish, so stupid and unsure, under his piercing gaze.

'Hello.' He didn't smile; nor did she expect him to. He looked. . .he looked wonderful, and it made Robyn feel ten times worse. 'Would you like some breakfast? Toast? Coffee?'

Robyn winced at the mention of food and swallowed gingerly. 'No, I. . . I don't feel up to eating anything.' She hesitated, then she asked, 'The jeep—can I phone the garage about getting it fixed?'

'Already done,' he announced briskly. 'They came over three hours ago and took it away.'

She should have felt happy, relieved—that was what she had wanted, wasn't it? But how eager he is to be rid of you, she thought, how desperate to have you out from under his roof. 'Oh, well, that's good. Thank you.' She tried to sound pleased, casual, anything except embarrassed and as miserable as she did now. 'When will it be ready? Did they say?'

'Around lunchtime,' he replied. 'They seemed to have a pretty good idea about what it might be. I asked them to return it as soon as they had done.'

'I see.' She hesitated, wondering what to do between now and the appearance of her get-away vehicle. Not stay here, in the house with him, that was for sure. She couldn't bear that! She glanced over at him again, struggling against the memories of last night, the way it had felt to have those strong, tanned hands touching her, caressing her. . .'I think I'll go out and do a bit more work,' she said into the silence that hung between them. 'I could do with some fresh air.'

'Are you OK, Robyn?' His words made her halt in the doorway. She turned, saw the small frown creasing his forehead. 'You do look pale.'

She swallowed again and tried to ignore the terrible sharp pain that was twisting viciously into the side of her head. 'Yes, yes of course I am,' she replied harshly, looking down. 'I just feel a bit sick, that's all!' She hardened her voice. 'It happens to women in my condition—remember?'

'Yes, of course,' he replied curtly, his expression neutral. 'I had forgotten.'

The fresh air was helping, but no amount of cool breeze or pleasant sunshine could take away the migraine that was fast developing. I should be inside, Robyn thought, lying down in a darkened room.

She made for the wood. It looked cool in there, peaceful, and it was as far away from Luke Denner and the barn as she could get. There would be a broken tree limb, she could sit quietly, think of other things. Forget.

It was difficult finding a way in. Years of neglect had led to tangles of trees and creepers and brambles. She skirted its edge and at last spotted a possible entry, finding a stick to whack at the jagged branches of an old dogrose. She glanced around her, instinctively assessing and planning how she would like this place to be. There was an old log and she sat down wearily, just glad of the quietness and the peace of her surroundings.

She had sat for maybe an hour, in an almost trancelike state, then she heard a rustling and approaching footsteps. She raised her head carefully, so as not to exacerbate the thundering over her eyes, and saw it was Luke.

'Your jeep has returned.'

'Good!' She got up gingerly and worked hard at appearing all right. 'Did they say what was wrong?'

'No, not that it would have made much sense if they had—I'm not a particular ace when it comes to car engines.'

'They gave you a bill, I presume?' she enquired. 'Did it cost a lot?'

He shrugged. 'Forget it; treat it as part-payment for expenses incurred or something.'

She shook her head and tried not to wince. 'No way; give it to me. I'll pay every last penny.'

'I said there was no need!' His voice matched hers. She saw the steely glint in his eyes.

'I don't care! Give it to me!' she repeated determinedly. She felt faint, nauseous. Blackness was swirling in and she fought against the need to clutch hold of something. 'It's my jeep, my responsibility. I don't want you bailing me out! I don't want your charity!'

'Funny,' he sneered, 'but I was under the impression that that's what you've been receiving ever since you made your dramatic appearance on Saturday!'

'Well, I'll pay, then!' she stormed. 'I'll pay for my board and lodging, for every damn thing! Now give me the bill!'

He thrust his hand casually into his jeans pocket and brought out a folded piece of paper. 'Have it your own way, then,' he said with an unperturbed shrug of his shoulders.

She snatched the paper from him and strode past. Her head was pounding dreadfully, and she had the awful sensation that she was going to actually throw up right in front of him.

She hurried too fast. Her foot caught on something, an old tree root, a bramble. Whatever it was, it sent her flying; one minute she was up, the next lying in an uncomfortable heap, half in, half out of a pile of brambles that was growing around the base of a tree in a haphazard, choking sort of way.

He was beside her in an instant, dragging the brambles away from her body, cursing furiously as the jagged thorns caught in her clothing. Gently he helped her up and Robyn saw the unmistakable frown of concern on his face. She had cut her arm. There were slivers of glass sparkling up at them from among the brambles. 'Let's get you back to the house,' he said quickly. 'I'll carry you.'

He had lifted her into his arms before she could protest, although in truth she hardly felt in any condition to trek back up the incline towards the barn.

When they were inside and once he had cleaned up the cut, he said, 'I'm getting a doctor.'

'It's nothing, just a gash. You've bandaged it. It will be OK.'

'For once in your life stop arguing!' he commanded. 'I'm calling the doctor whether you like it or not!'

She gave up. She felt too unwell to pursue the point any longer, and, besides, maybe the doctor could give her something for her migraine.

He arrived about an hour later, brisk and elderly with very little bedside manner.

'So, young lady, been falling over, have we?' He removed the bandage that Luke had put around her arm—already it was quite heavily stained with blood. 'Mmm, needs a couple of stitches,' he remarked, rummaging in his bag. 'Just whip these in and then we'll have a good look at you. Your friend tells me there might be complications—you fell heavily, didn't you?'

'Not too badly,' Robyn murmured. 'There was some glass, that was all. There's no need to worry,' she insisted, once he'd finished with his hideous needle and thread. 'Really, I'm OK!'

The doctor gave her a cool smile. 'Well, I think that's for me to decide, don't you?' he remarked mildly. 'Now, how many weeks pregnant are you?'

Robyn swallowed and blanched. Oh, God! Pregnant! That was why Luke had looked so tense, she'd forgotten. 'I'm. . . I'm not pregnant,' she said quietly.

The doctor gave her a puzzled look, withdrawing the light he was flashing into her eyes for a moment. 'But your friend said. . .'

'He's made a mistake!' Robyn retorted.

'But he's obviously got the idea from somewhere,' the doctor replied insistently. 'Are you sure. . .?'

'Of course I'm sure!' Robyn said in a low voice. 'I'm positively, absolutely not pregnant! I've got a bad migraine, I tripped and fell and cut my arm. End of story.'

The doctor looked down thoughtfully at her, considered a moment and then placed a firm hand on her forehead. 'You feel a little warm,' he murmured. 'I'll give you some tablets, they'll help you to relax.' He got up and clicked his briefcase shut. 'Take two now and then make sure you rest—you'll be fine in a couple of hours.'

When Luke came in she was still fuming. 'You had no right!' she declared heatedly. 'No right at all!'

'To do what?' He threw her a cool, quizzical look.

'To inform that doddering old fool that I was pregnant!' she snapped. 'It's none of your business!'

'He needed to know,' he replied coolly. 'You didn't seem yourself and you fell awkwardly; I thought it might be overlooked.'

'Overlooked! You think something as important as that would slip my mind? If I were carrying a baby, don't you think it would be my first priority!'

'If?' He turned sharply from the french window and the view he had been looking at so intently. 'What's that supposed to mean, Robyn?'

She hesitated and shifted nervously on the settee, rubbing a weary hand over her eyes, 'I'm not pregnant.'

'Since when?'

'Since never!' She glared at him, fighting the dull ache in her head, 'I never was. You got it wrong.'

Robyn saw the tightness in his expression, the grim set of his jaw and began to scramble up from her half-lying position on the settee. 'I'm going home,' she declared. 'I'll send the money to cover the bill.'

'Stay exactly where you are!' he rasped. 'Don't you dare move a muscle!'

She hesitated, and didn't. It would have been more than her life was worth.

He came up to her, and she saw his expression of controlled ferocity at close quarters. 'So why the game?' he enquired, with menacing quietness.

'There was no game.' Robyn's face contorted with the effort of appearing calm. 'You assumed and I chose not to enlighten you, that's all.'

'That's all?' His eyes pierced hers. 'Do you know how

concerned I've been about you and this damn phantom baby?' He grasped her by the shoulders, his fingers biting in, through the thinness of her top. 'Well, do you?'

Robyn summoned up every ounce of strength and hate and found she still didn't have enough to cope with Luke's overwhelming anger and her migraine all at the same time. He had been concerned for her. The novel thought penetrated and stayed with her. 'No,' she mumbled, sagging suddenly, so that if it hadn't have been for his firm grip she probably would have sunk to the ground, 'I didn't think. I. . .'

He propelled her away from him and Robyn struggled to stay upright. 'No!' he repeated derisively, turning back towards the window. 'You very rarely do—do you? Your whole life's spent in one long thoughtless whirl, I should imagine. Letting me believe you were pregnant! Quite amusing, was it? Letting me think that you slept with so many men you didn't have the first idea who the father was!'

'You were willing to believe it!' Robyn stormed, eyes blazing. She went over to where he was standing, looking him right in the eyes so that he could see how furious she was. 'You were already convinced, even before you asked me! How do you think that made me feel?'

Luke studied her, his eyes raking her face. 'I haven't the first idea,' he said in deliberate clipped tones. Then he added, 'Well, at least you're a clever girl; you take precautions and you're not pregnant—that's something, I suppose.'

'You bastard!' Robyn's hand came up, but he was, as usual, too quick for her. His grip was like iron bands around her wrist, his face was as black as thunder, his eyes. . . God, they were like ice and yet fiery all at the same time.

'Always the childish option, Robyn,' he sneered. 'How very predictable you can be at times.'

Robyn was trembling so hard that she could barely breathe. His body was up against hers, close and strong and totally in control. She could feel the roughness of his denims against her slim thighs, feel the broadness of his chest against her own. I'm a fool, she thought tearfully, knowing the very last vestiges of the shaky companionship they shared were gone for good. I've probably finished what little chance I had of getting out of here in one piece.

He glared down at her for eternal seconds and then his mouth descended and Robyn felt the anger and fire, still there, but focused this time in the searing heat of his kiss, the grip of his embrace, the rough glory as his hands roamed her body, conjuring desire and need out of nowhere, moulding her to him, showing Robyn just how much she wanted him, how much he desired her. Luke was in command and this time instinct told Robyn there would be no withdrawal, no respite from his sexual onslaught, from the tension that had been building between them since the very first moment. He wanted her, just as she wanted him. This time there could be only one conclusion.

His hands were exploring her body, impatient hands that lifted the T-shirt and flicked expertly at the catch of her bra. Robyn gasped and felt the sharp ache deep in the pit of her stomach, as his hands covered both breasts, moulding and squeezing, gasped again as she felt his lips following his touch and she felt the pull of his mouth, sucking and probing at each aroused nipple.

'Robyn.' His voice, husky, urgent against her skin, told her all she needed to know. His mouth plundered hers, brushing her lips, forcing entry with his tongue, demanding, demanding all the while. For reply Robyn ran her hands instinctively across his chest, down and down to the waist of his jeans, further to his inner thigh, to the place where his need was strongest.

He lifted her then, in one swift movement, and carried her to the sofa, laying her back, murmuring her name over and over, kissing again, consuming her with a passion that thrilled and left Robyn weak and yet powerful all at the same time, because she could do this to him—she could make Luke Denner groan with desire and need. Hurriedly he removed her clothes, his own shirt, his jeans. And then he was with her, kneeling over her, expertly discarding the lacy panties, stroking her body, finding the place that strengthened Robyn's need, lingering, almost torturing her with longing. She had never imagined it would feel so wonderful, so right. She was desperate for more of him; her body ached for fulfilment, for the feel of his need and strength inside— so that when he entered her, when she felt that first wondrous thrust, which brought both pleasure and pain, it was as she'd always dreamed, and as his urgent rhythm continued, bringing them both to that glorious peak of exhilaration, Robyn cried out his name, held him close to her for a moment and wished things could be like this forever.

'Robyn. Hey, what's the matter? Look at me; don't turn away.' Luke's hand gently stroked the curls from her face. She could feel the warmth of his breath on her cheek as he spoke, the hammering of his heart against her. 'Robyn?'

She wriggled up, away, trying to hide her nakedness from him, groping for her clothes, avoiding his look, his touch.

He sat up, naked and at ease, handing the swiftly discarded T-shirt to her from the floor, watching while she scrambled self-consciously into her clothes with an expression that Robyn didn't dare to read.

'I've got to go.' Robyn rummaged frantically around for her shoes.

'Why?' he asked quietly, with a voice that held no emotion. 'Why have you got to go?'

Robyn darted a look at the strong impassive face and swallowed. 'Because. . .because I must.'

He let out a breath, deep and controlled. 'You regret us making love?' It was half-statement, half-question.

Robyn paused, pressed her lips together tightly and then continued tying her trainers with shaking fingers.

'Well?' he demanded suddenly, and now there was a hint of savagery in his tone. 'Answer me!'

'It was a mistake,' Robyn whispered. 'We got carried away, we didn't know what we were——'

'Don't you dare!' He grabbed her, reaching over to where she sat at the end of the sofa, turning her roughly by the arm so that she had to face him, had to look deep into his angry, ice-blue eyes. 'A mistake?' he repeated scornfully. 'We didn't know what we were doing? My God!' He shook his head in furious disbelief and Robyn felt herself tremble as he ran his fingers through his hair in a gesture of fury. 'I don't understand you, Robyn. . .' His voice trailed away and then hardened again. 'And you obviously don't understand me!' He thrust his face close, covered her mouth with his lips for a moment in a searing kiss, just to remind her. 'When I make love, believe me, it's no mistake, Robyn. I wanted you and you wanted me. We made love and it was good. Very spec——'

'Don't!' Robyn backed away, tearing her arm from his hold, and scrambled to her feet, shaking. 'Can't you see that I don't want to talk about it? It happened, but it. . .it wasn't meant to!'

She moved blindly to the door, gripping the handle until her knuckles whitened. She knew she was handling this badly, acting like a fool, making a scene because she couldn't face the pretence, couldn't face having to stifle her feelings, her crazy and immature hopes—hopes that would always be doomed to failure where a man like Luke Denner was concerned. The touch of him, the taste of him, the moment of his possession had been glorious, a very, very special moment in her life. But then a man like Luke Denner knew that! Surely he did?

She turned and faced him, forcing herself to meet his steady, almost unbelieving gaze. 'You know,' she said quietly, 'that I've never slept with any man until today.'

And then, with a final click of the door, she left.

CHAPTER EIGHT

'FOR heaven's sakes, Robyn!' Anne snapped. 'Will you stop this pathetic charade of pretending nothing's the matter? I know it's him, this man—what was his name?— Luke Denner, that's got you so worked up; you've not been the same since those few days in the country and that plan of his has been sitting on your desk untouched for days on end. I thought this latest project was supposed to be the breakthrough you were looking for!'

'It was,' Robyn replied miserably.

'Well, whatever's happened, for God's sake stop taking your frustrations out on me. I'm absolutely sick of your moods. Phone him, see him, sort something out and then perhaps we'll be able to have a normal conversation without you snapping my head off!'

Robyn took a deep breath and glanced at her friend. She had never experienced Anne's anger before. It was quite a shock. Robyn bit worriedly at her lip. She had been thinking about nothing else except this phone call for days now, wrestling with the conflict of emotions that were raging inside. Part of her, that stubborn, spirited side, the side that had got her into this mess in the first place, wouldn't let her give up, back out and admit that Luke Denner and his sexuality were more than she could handle. It was pride, she supposed; deep down the prospect of fading away, giving up, was just as terrifying as seeing Luke Denner again.

'Go on!' Anne encouraged. 'The telephone won't bite. Just pick up the receiver and get it over with.'

It was ringing. Robyn clutched the receiver and found she didn't have the first idea of what she would say when he answered it. I've dialled too quickly, she thought. I need to rehearse, get it clear in my mind. But then, just as she had decided to abandon the attempt and risk Anne's annoyance, he answered, repeating the number in a cool, clear, frighteningly strong voice.

Robyn took a gulp, swore she wouldn't gabble and then proceeded to do just that 'Umm—hello, this is Robyn. I'm phoning to arrange a time. . . I mean—um—I'm phoning to let you know, because I've finished the plans and I didn't know whether to send them or——'

She cringed at the sound of her own voice and took a breath. Professional businesswoman? Who was she kidding?

'It's been over two weeks. What took you so long?'

One classic Luke Denner sentence—no greeting, no pleasantries. That was all it took. She was angry all over again.

'I do have other clients,' she declared irritably. 'I can't abandon everything just like that!'

'If you remember, Robyn,' he replied crisply, 'I did say that I wanted this work completed by the end of the summer. Time is passing by; this doesn't leave much leeway, if your plans——'

'Prove to be unsuitable?' Robyn finished for him. 'I suppose I might have expected you to remind me of that possibility!'

'Don't interrupt, Robyn,' he drawled, with infuriating calm. 'Hasn't anyone told you it's not very polite? I was about to say, before you jumped down my throat, if your plans need altering in any way.'

'I won't allow them to be altered!' Robyn shot back, furious with herself for giving him the opportunity to make her feel foolish and inferior all over again. 'They're as I want them. I've put a lot of time and effort into them and I'll not allow you or anyone else to change them!'

'That's absolutely ridiculous, Robyn, and you know it!' His voice was quiet, not like her own, which had been rising with every syllable, but he was angry all the same, she could feel it, even down the miles of telephone cable that separated them.

'Well, if you think it's ridiculous, then so be it!' she cried, determinedly adding more fuel to the fire. 'But it's how I feel about these plans, now, after. . .' she faltered a second and then forced herself on '. . .after everything. Either you accept them as they are, or you reject them completely.'

What I am saying? she thought wildly, aware of the thumping beat of her heart, the tension in her whole body as she gripped the phone and waited for his curt reply.

There was a silence. Robyn wondered whether he'd simply put the receiver down without her realising and walked away. If that had happened, then what would she do? 'So. . .so I'll send them, shall I?' she asked, holding her breath, bracing herself, waiting for the blunt, 'You do that!' the violent, 'Go to Hell!' the indifferent dismissal, or, even worse, the continuing silence which meant he had really hung up on her.

'Taking the easy way out again, Robyn?' he sneered, making her jump violently after the empty silence. 'Oh, no! You'll bring them,' he ordered harshly. 'Plans without the designer are no use to me. Tomorrow at three. Be there!'

And with that he replaced the receiver with a sharp, impatient click.

'So what's the verdict?' Anne asked cheerily, a moment later. 'I bet it wasn't as bad as all that!'

Robyn looked up from her position on the floor by the phone. 'Worse,' she muttered, 'much worse.'

Anne raised her eyebrows in surprise. 'Surely not,' she said lightly. 'I thought this latest project had you all excited—wasn't it your big opportunity to prove yourself?'

'I believed so—in the beginning,' Robyn agreed quietly.

'But not now?' Anne asked. 'Come on, Robyn, tell me! It's like getting blood out of a stone!'

Robyn hesitated. Oh, to blurt it all out. To tell Anne everything, to relieve herself of some of the misery. But she couldn't. What had happened was still too new, too vividly painful. 'We just don't get on,' Robyn declared neutrally. 'He's angry and irritable and he's made it clear from the very beginning that he doesn't expect me to come up to scratch.'

'Well, well,' Anne remarked, 'so that's why you were

reticent about your stay in the Cotswolds. I thought you were a bit depressed when you returned.'

A bit? Robyn thought, remembering the way she had flung herself out of the house, the agony of driving home, the touch and taste of him haunting her down every mile of motorway. . .the floods of tears. . .

'But you haven't cancelled?' Anne asked.

'No!' Robyn replied with fire in her eyes. 'Oh, no. I'm going through with this until the end.'

'Good girl!' Anne applauded. 'That's the spirit! Why let a mean old duffer like this Mr Denner kill all your self-confidence?'

What self-confidence! Robyn thought later as she stared at her reflection in the dressing-table mirror and forced herself to imagine what tomorrow's meeting with Luke would actually feel like. You've got to go through with it, she told herself. You've got to face him, show him you're a big girl. But I'm more than a big girl, she cried silently, gazing at her face, devoid now of any make-up. I may look like a child, but Luke—Luke changed all that. Inside I'm a woman.

Robyn unscrewed a jar of moisturiser and smoothed it over her face and neck. The idea had been in the back of her mind for a few days now and this evening had decided it for sure. With a resolute nod at her reflection, she turned away from the bouncing curls and lightly freckled face and began to undress for bed.

Everywhere glamorous women! Or at least that was the way it seemed. Robyn strolled up the shopping mall with its glass and fancy tiles and green lush plants, which gave it the strange appearance of a tropical jungle littered with high-street stores, and considered which one of the high-class boutiques she should enter first. This was going to be a big step. Her hard-fought for earnings were at stake here as well as her own self-confidence—she had to get it right.

The black trousers caught her eye first, displayed catchingly in the window on a mannequin with the same colour hair as her own. Robyn ventured closer and considered. They were silky and well cut and they would be the perfect start from which to build her new image. She took a deep breath, forced herself not to feel intimidated by the exceptionally well-groomed woman who had just entered the boutique, and ventured in.

Almost one hour later she emerged. Incredibly she had found not only helpful assistants who took delight in helping her, but all that she wanted in that one shop. Three outfits costing an amount of money that didn't bear thinking about, but which were nevertheless perfect. They transformed her.

Another hour and her new image was almost complete. She'd bought an array of stylish cosmetics, received a free lesson on how to apply all her expensive purchases from one of the white-coated assistants in the department store, bought shoes and bags and accessories, flashed her friendly credit card until she thought the plastic might melt from overuse—and now the finishing and most dramatic change of all!

Robyn paid the bill, smiled her thanks and emerged feeling curiously light-headed.

As she strolled past the shop windows she ran her fingers through the short layered style that the hairdresser had said was made for her, and felt like someone else.

'Robyn! Your hair!'

Anne's first words were not uttered in the encouraging tones Robyn had hoped for. Anne came into the kitchen, dumped her handbag on to the table and gawped in astonishment. 'All your beautiful curls—they've gone.'

Robyn looked up from the kitchen sink and placed a washed plate on to the draining-board. 'Yes, I had noticed,' she murmured drily. 'Well, don't just stand there, say something—like it's wonderful, fabulous!' She grinned. 'Only phrases along those lines are acceptable!'

Anne sat down with her elbows on the table and considered. 'It will take a bit of getting used to,' she remarked slowly, 'although,' she added after a slight pause, 'it does make you look——'

'Older?' Robyn interrupted eagerly. 'Please say it does! Please say that I finally look my age at least!'

Anne smiled and shook her head. 'You're mad, do you know that? But actually. . .' she considered some more '. . .yes, you do; in fact everything about you looks quite, quite different. Take that pinny off. What are you wearing underneath?'

Robyn whisked away the apron and gave a twirl. 'Oh, yes!' Anne murmured encouragingly. 'Now that is smart!'

Robyn glowed and smiled and felt more confident. 'I've bought a couple more outfits, a smart black dress, some good trousers,' she said eagerly. 'My make-up's faded a lot now, but when everything's together I look well, I look pretty good actually.'

'So you feel happier about yourself?' Anne asked.

'Yes, yes, I think I do,' Robyn replied seriously. 'This look is what I had in mind.'

'And do you think he'll like it?' Anne asked, with an innocent expression.

Robyn sank her hands back into the soapy water again. 'Who?' she murmured, conjuring up tones of equal innocence.

Anne giggled. 'You know very well who!' she accused. 'Mr Denner, of course! Do you know I lay awake for a little while last night and came to the conclusion that I had no grounds for thinking him old or frumpy? In fact I don't know what made me think he was that way in the first place—unless it was you, of course, leading me off the trail! So come on, Robyn, tell me—how old is this Mr Denner? What does he look like?'

'Oh, I'm not sure,' Robyn replied vaguely, looking away out of the window. 'Thirty-one, something like that.'

'Tall? Blond? Dark?' Anne asked, her eyes gleaming with curiosity.

'Tall, over six feet, dark hair, blue eyes,' Robyn murmured hurriedly.

'Wow!' Anne exclaimed. 'And stunningly good-looking of course?' she persisted.

'Superficially, I suppose,' Robyn conceded reluctantly. 'Some women would find him attractive.'

'But you don't?'

Robyn turned and faced Anne. 'Whether I find him attractive is neither here nor there. We fought like cat and dog the whole time we were together—or at least most of the time,' she added, remembering, 'he made my life an absolute misery!'

'You sound bitter,' Anne remarked with an expression of surprise. 'Not like you to let someone get under your skin.'

'I know.' Robyn gave a small sigh and pulled off her rubber gloves. 'I'm sorry, Anne, if I've been taking it out on you these past couple of weeks.' She glanced at her watch. 'Look, I'm going now; I've got to be at his place for three.' She pulled a face. 'Wish me luck, won't you? I've got a terrible feeling that I'm going to need it!'

The jeep undoubtedly did not live up to her new image. Robyn smiled to herself as she charged down the motorway and imagined how she must look in such a battered, ramshackle old thing.

Halfway there and she felt like a break. She pulled in at a motorway service station and decided on lunch. She bent to retrieve her bag from where it had fallen under the seat and saw the parcel which made her heart sink. Oh, no! Anne's mother! Or rather her birthday present! Robyn cursed her own forgetfulness and pulled it out. Anne had given her the parcel to post two days ago and she had completely forgotten all about it. How could she have done such a thing? Robyn looked at the careful wrapping, Anne's neat writing, and sighed. It was her mother's fiftieth birthday, quite a milestone, and Anne had emphasised how much she wanted it to get there on time. Typical of you, Robyn, she muttered. Full of good intentions that never quite go right!

She bit her lip and considered, consulting her trusty road atlas. She had given herself a fair amount of time to get to Luke's, and if she left the motorway at the next junction and didn't hang around she'd be only a little late at the most. But to be late again, even if it was only by an hour or so, was just the start she didn't want. He would have another excuse to berate her.

But this is your fault, she told herself. Anne trusted you with the parcel; the least you can do is make sure it reaches its destination on time.

Robyn arrived at Luke's later than she had expected—far later—flustered and hot from busy traffic and wrongly taken turns, tense as the prospect of seeing Luke again became reality.

Anne's mother and father had been delighted to see her, plying her with tea and cake and endless conversation in the delightful setting of their Oxfordshire home. But they had kept her too long and she hadn't wanted to appear rude because they were nice people, and now she was very, very late.

Robyn headed the jeep up the by now familiar track to the barn and tried to get herself into the right frame of mind. Poise was going to be the order of the day—poise and sophistication; she had taken great care to look the part, now all she had to do was feel that way too.

There were cars, many of them, along the track, parked in a haphazard sort of way. Robyn slowed the jeep with a puzzled frown, considering. Luke hadn't mentioned company, she thought, but then he wasn't expecting her at this ungodly hour—it was nearly eight already.

I can't turn back, she thought; I can't go through all this again. She took a resolute breath and manoeuvred the jeep behind a low sports car. It would be now or never. He was here, expecting her; she would get this ordeal over and done with.

Robyn straightened her dress, glanced in the rear-view mirror at her still unrecognisable appearance and got out.

There was the deep throb of music coming from the barn, the unmistakable noise of many lively conversations. Robyn weaved her way through the cars and forced herself to walk confidently up to the front door, despite the sinking feeling in her stomach. Don't be a wimp, she thought. Be confident! You haven't even got over the first hurdle yet and you're ready to quit! What does it matter that he's cold and unforgiving and hateful? That you have the most God-awful rows? That the last time you saw him he made love to you?

Guests spilled noisily out through the open french windows, couples laughed and shrieked and danced and embraced intimately.

He was having one hell of a party.

Robyn took a deep breath and gave a half-hearted knock at the front door. No one would hear her, but she couldn't face having to find him among this unfamiliar crowd. Better to knock and hope someone would come to her aid.

Someone did.

'Well, this is rather nice! A lovely late arrival.'

Robyn turned and saw a tall blond man with a smiling mouth strolling casually towards her. 'I don't think there's any point in knocking,' he murmured, putting a casual arm around Robyn's shoulders. 'Come round this way—I'll get you a drink.'

'Umm—well, no thanks.' Robyn smiled nervously. 'You see, I'm not a guest; I'm here on business—to see Mr Denner.'

'Really?' He raised intrigued eyebrows and kept his arm exactly where it was. 'Well, lucky old Luke! Would you like me to find him for you? I'm sure he's in there somewhere, surrounded by a quite unfair bevy of beauties. I'm Callum, by the way.'

Robyn smiled up at him, pleased that she should be rescued by such a friendly and not unattractive individual. 'I'm Robyn,' she said with a cheerful smile. 'Pleased to meet you.'

'Likewise,' he grinned, and proffered the glass he was holding. 'Here, have a drink anyway, while I go and find Luke. I won't be a minute.'

She hovered uncertainly near the front door, clasping the glass, feeling foolish with her long scroll of plans and her hammering heart.

She wondered how he would be, whether she'd cope, what she would say, and had just decided to rehearse an opening line when, with a jolt deep in the pit of her stomach, she saw him, weaving through the clusters of people, coming towards her, looking, as always, more handsome than she remembered, dressed in dark, well-cut trousers and a crisp white shirt that revealed just a glimpse of his tanned chest, the strength of dark matted hair.

'You're late!'

Robyn's heart dived. 'Yes,' she replied coolly, 'I know.'

'Very late,' he persisted, flicking cool, unfriendly eyes over her.

Robyn met his insolent gaze and felt the hackles rising. 'I realise that!' she replied. 'I don't need you to point out the obvious.'

'So what was so pressing you couldn't be here on time?' he enquired sarcastically. 'An earthquake, invasion of hostile forces, or did the jeep just break down again?'

Robyn raised the glass to her lips and took a first sip; she had a feeling that counting to ten was not going to work, but she tried it all the same.

'So am I going to be rewarded with an explanation,' he growled, 'or are you just going to stand there sipping that damn punch all evening?'

Robyn looked up and forced a sarcastic smile. 'Well, isn't this nice!' she murmured brightly. 'Do you know all the way here I've been looking forward to your particular brand of polite conversation? Such a change from the predictable pleasantries and good manners that some people feel they have to indulge in.'

'Cut the sarcasm, Robyn,' he growled. 'I'm in no mood!'

'Oh, I can see that!' Robyn snapped. 'Your thunderous expression has a curious habit of giving everything away.'

She took a deep breath. This wasn't right! She had planned on being ultra-cool, whatever provocation he might throw at her, and yet at the first word here she was letting him get to her all over again! She swallowed and with monumental effort said, 'Look, I'm sorry I'm late. Something came up. . .'

'You could have phoned,' he commented. 'That's the usual thing. Phoned and explained—or would that have been too simple?'

'Yes, yes, I know, but. . .' The truth was she hadn't been able to face it. She couldn't face speaking to him down the wires of a telephone again, not after yesterday, and, besides, he might have cancelled their arrangement and she hadn't wanted that.

'Well?' He was deliberately making it hard for her. She could tell, just by the glint in his eyes, the fearsome expression on his face.

'Look, I'm here now,' she replied, in quite amazing conciliatory tones, 'and I have apologised.'

'And you think I should be satisfied with that?' he enquired coldly, dark brows raised.

'Most other people would be!' she flashed back irritably.

'Well, I'm not most other people, am I?' he snarled. 'I demand a lot more from my employees.'

Employees? God! she thought. What an arrogant, unfeeling swine! 'Here!'

She thrust the plans towards him. 'Take these, for God's sake! Look at them and then, if by some miracle you're happy with them, let me know. I'm not staying around just so you can use me as your verbal punch-bag again. I've had enough!'

She moved as if to go by him, but he stuck out a hand and grabbed her arm.

'You're not going anywhere,' he snapped. 'I want you to go over these plans with me.'

Robyn gave him a hard look. 'Is there any point?' she asked. 'We both know you're going to reject them out of hand! I'd be wasting my time—and yours!' she added bitterly.

'Who said anything about rejecting them out of hand?' he said evenly. 'If they're up to standard and I like them, I'll use them—simple as that.'

She glared at him unbelievingly. What a rat! God! How he twisted things to suit himself! she thought angrily. 'And you expect me to believe you?' she asked incredulously. 'After the things you said?'

'Yes. Oh, come on, Robyn,' he added, when she shook her head in disbelief and looked away. 'Stop being so petulant! I was mad then, very mad—with myself, with you. People have been known to say things they don't mean when they're angry—you of all people should know by now that I'm no exception to that rule.'

'Oh, I know that!' Robyn retorted. 'Only too well!'

There was silence, filled only by the glare of expression, the tension that sparked between them, just as it always had, always would as long as they lived and breathed.

Luke let out a deep breath and ran a hand through his thick hair in the familiar gesture of exasperation. 'We're at it again, aren't we, Robyn?' he remarked ruefully.

Robyn watched his expression, saw the relaxation of his features, and breathed an inward sigh of relief. She nodded and found her mouth had twisted into a smile. 'Yes,' she murmured, and added hurriedly, 'Look, I really didn't mean to be quite so late, but I had to——'

He raised a hand. 'It's OK. You don't have to explain. I lost my temper; I thought something might have happened to you, that was all. I tried to phone your place, but there was no reply.'

'You were worried?' Robyn blurted, aware of a great leap of pleasure. He smiled. 'Of course I was worried! You and that jeep—what a lethal combination.' He pulled an expression of mock horror. 'I could picture you so clearly, hurling yourselves down the motorway.' Robyn smiled and he added, lowering his voice, 'About last time—the way we parted. . .'

'Don't, Luke,' Robyn pleaded, shaking her head. 'I'd rather not.'

'But Robyn, we can't just leave things. . .'

'We can,' she insisted. 'Please, Luke.' She turned and threw him a desperate look. 'That's the way I want it— honestly.'

He paused, regarding her with intense blue eyes. 'Can I say then that I'm sorry? Sorry for the way I behaved, for the way that we parted?'

It was happening again. He hadn't read the script, wasn't acting as she had envisaged. An apology? One that sounded both gentle and completely sincere? 'I'm sorry too,' Robyn whispered faintly, staring down at her hands. 'Luke, it's OK.' She let out a deep, shaky breath. 'Look, can we just put that behind us now? Get on with the work?'

He gave a wry smile and she saw that the expression on his face was one of acceptance. 'We can try,' he replied, 'if that's what you want.' He smiled down at her. 'So let's see your finished plan. I liked your ideas; I made that clear before, didn't I? So unless you've put in something totally hideous like an ornamental fountain slap bang in the middle of the wildflower meadow,' he teased, 'or designed a terrace that has multi-coloured crazy paving——'

'As if I would!' Robyn cut in waspishly.

'Well, there you are, then!' Luke replied. 'Nothing to worry about! Now come with me,' he ordered, throwing her an attractive curl of a smile. 'You're just the excuse I need.'

She looked at him sharply, finally found the good sense to tug her arm out of his hold. 'Excuse?'

'Yes, this party.' He turned and looked around him. 'If you remember I'm not particularly fond of them,' he murmured, 'especially when they're in my own home; I prefer to keep well away.'

'So why have one, then?' Robyn enquired bluntly. 'Rather masochistic, isn't it?'

'Well, it would be, if I had arranged it,' he replied. 'What you see all around is the result of a group of well-meaning friends who happened upon the mistaken idea of a surprise get-together—they turned up about an hour ago with boxes full of food and a quite amazing selection of drink.'

'You had absolutely no idea?' Robyn asked, with undisguised curiosity.

'None whatsoever,' he drawled, eyeing the lively antics that were taking place a few yards from them. 'Do you think I would have waited around for all this if I had?'

'You are a misery, do you know that?' Robyn retorted with spirit. 'They've probably all gone to a lot of trouble.'

'Tough! I'm going to give them another hour and then that's it—they can all go home. Now I'm going to go inside and get myself a drink,' he announced, 'and then we are going to go over to the far field where there's a modicum of peace and we are going to look at these plans together, OK?'

She waited nervously while he went inside, and wondered how things were going to turn out. She glanced down at her new, stylish dress, ran her fingers through her shorn tresses and remembered all the effort she had gone to. What a fool you are, Robyn Drew! she muttered fiercely. He hasn't even noticed.

He emerged then and she dropped her hand self-consciously, straightened her dress and tried to rearrange her expression into one of indifferent professionalism as an attractive blonde girl draped herself decorously around his neck and began to kiss him with quite unnecessary passion.

Robyn watched under the guise of taking a sip from her glass, saw the casual way he bent to kiss her, the commanding dismissal, and wished she didn't feel quite so. . .so embarrassed—No, damn it, dismayed—by what she saw. You're being silly, she told herself; a man as attractive as Luke Denner would be bound to have many women in his life, any number of girlfriends; hadn't she schooled herself into thinking this at least a hundred times—ever since that very first meeting, ever since he had dragged her unceremoniously into that small, chaste bedroom, ever since he had made love to her?

'Ready?' he asked.

She followed him into the field and they sat beneath the shade of a large oak tree. Robyn laid the plans out on the grass and knelt beside them. She cleared her throat nervously and was just about to launch into a business like explanation when he said suddenly, 'So what's with the altered image?'

Robyn blushed, darted a quick look at him and then gave a nonchalant shrug. 'I just felt like a bit of a change, that's all.'

'More like a full metamorphosis,' he drawled, leaning

back against the huge, craggy trunk of the tree and gazing at her with wicked eyes. 'Rather sudden, wasn't it?'

'Yes, I suppose you could say that.' She looked across and tried to appear careless about the whole thing. 'I was sick of the old me—too predictable.'

He gave a short, amused laugh. 'You? Predictable? Are you kidding?'

'I was talking appearances,' Robyn retorted, 'and you know it!'

'Of course it makes you look a lot older,' he added thoughtfully.

Robyn felt a flush of unguarded satisfaction. 'Does it?' she asked swiftly. 'Does it really?'

His lips curved into a smile and immediately she realised her mistake. 'No,' he replied, 'I lied. I'm afraid as far as I'm concerned you still look about sixteen. But ten out of ten for effort, Robyn; you do look very smart—I hardly recognised you.'

Robyn ground her teeth together and glared at him. 'Don't patronise me, Luke,' she snapped. 'That's the last thing I need. Why don't you just come right out and say I look ridiculous? Don't break a habit of a lifetime and hold back on my account!'

He gave a throaty laugh. 'Tut-tut, do I detect someone fishing for compliments?' he asked. 'Actually, I really do think you look good; that hairstyle does suit you—makes you look quite elfin-like.'

Robyn snorted impatiently and threw him a look of disgust. 'Elfin-like?' she queried. 'What sort of a description is that? Am I supposed to be flattered by the fact that you think I resemble a small magical creature, who, as far as my childhood recollections goes, always wears a stupid hat and has pointed ears?'

'I said elfin, Robyn,' he corrected, 'not elf—it does have slightly different connotations.'

'Not as far as I'm concerned,' she retorted. 'Pixie, elf, elfin—they're all the same to me! Look,' she added sharply, aware of her pink cheeks and his mocking expression, 'I came all the way here to work, not to be insulted by you about my appearance, and I'd like to get on, the light's beginning to fade—is that all right with you?'

'Suits me just fine,' he drawled lazily. 'Don't let it be said I stopped anyone working—especially Robyn Drew,' he added sarcastically.

He came closer and sat beside her on the grass, close, so that she could hardly concentrate on what she was supposed to be saying. Robyn cleared her throat awkwardly and tried to muster a voice that sounded as if she was in total control. 'I'll begin with the wood,' she said, pointing to the plan. 'I've created a series of paths that lead through and around, and there will be mass underplanting of natural flowers—bluebells, snowdrops, that sort of thing. In time it will come to look very beautiful. . .'

He allowed her to go through everything without so much as a single interruption. It seemed too good to be true and when Robyn had said all that was necessary she sat back and eyed him with suspicion.

'What's that look for?' he asked. 'I haven't said a word!'

'That's just it,' Robyn murmured. 'Why so silent? Most clients have usually chipped in with some comment by now.'

He rose to his feet. 'Ah, but I'm not most clients!' He held out his hand. 'Come on, let's brave the barn. I'll get you a drink—you must be in dire need of one, after all that talking!'

Robyn looked up at him, at his outstretched hand, and wished, not for the first time, that she knew what was going on in his mind. Had she done OK? Did he like the design?

'When are you going to let me know?' she asked, clasping his hand, allowing herself the fleeting pleasure of his touch. 'About the plan, I mean.'

He pulled her up to her feet. 'I've already decided,' he replied. 'I thought that much was obvious.'

'Not to me,' Robyn murmured, hardly daring to hope that his lighter mood might have something to do with the fact that he really did like her work.

He smiled and pulled her close with one swift jerk of

his wrist. 'Your design is very, very good,' he told her smoothly, curving his free hand under her chin, so that she had to look directly into his eyes. 'Better than I ever imagined.'

She heard his words and felt the surge of long-awaited satisfaction.

'You've proved me wrong,' he murmured quietly. 'How does it feel?'

Robyn was suddenly finding breathing quite a problem; she wasn't sure if she was anywhere near able to reply—not when he looked at her like that, not when his body was so close to hers. 'V-very good,' she managed at last, desperately aware of the way his fingers were creeping from her chin, sliding down lightly to her neck, then on towards her throat—the ghost of a touch, as light and sensual as any touch could be and all the more powerful and disturbing for that. She swallowed, struggling against the overwhelming desire to allow his hands to continue, but knowing that if she did. . .if she did. . . 'It feels very good indeed,' she added croakily.

'You mean this?' He traced a delicate figure of eight across the smooth pale skin at her shoulders. 'You have wonderful skin, Robyn,' he murmured huskily. 'Quite, quite beautiful, like porcelain.' He stroked some more, the tips of his fingers just skimming beneath the wide straps, at the edges of the scooped neckline, teasing, tormenting. . .

'What you said last time, just before you left. . .' he murmured. 'You don't know how——'

'Well, there you are!' Melissa's high-pitched voice carried irritatingly on the warm night air.

Luke uttered a curse under his breath and swung around, dropping Robyn's hand, which he still held, like a stone. 'What the hell does she want?' he asked of no one in particular as Melissa approached, a vision in pale lilac.

'Luke, darling,' she simpered, winding a thin, heavily tanned arm around Luke's waist, 'we've been looking all over for you, you naughty boy!' She cast suspicious, icy eyes at Robyn, a what-are-you-doing-here look, and continued, 'Now come with me back to the barn—we have a little surprise for you.'

'Another, Melissa?' Luke drawled, allowing a weary sigh to escape from his lips. 'Are you sure I'll be able to stand all this excitement in one evening?'

'Now don't be difficult, darling!' Melissa cajoled. 'Just follow me please! It will be more than my life's worth if I let you get away again.'

Robyn followed as a determined Melissa led Luke, whose expression resembled that of a prisoner about to be given his last rites, across the field and in through the french windows.

The guests, packed cheek by jowl, parted as he entered, and suddenly she knew the reason for the party. A discordant and high-spirited version of an old tune rang out into the evening air. It was his birthday.

'Enjoy that, did you?' he drawled a little while later, reappearing with a plate piled high with soft sponge and cream and two glasses that overflowed with bubbling champagne.

'Every bit,' Robyn agreed. 'Especially the part where you blew out the candles—very amiable of you, I thought.

'Considering I'm such a miserable, ungrateful bastard, you mean?' he enquired drily.

'Precisely,' she replied. 'I was completely overcome with the emotion of the occasion. You played your part well.'

'Ah, well, your little lecture must have had some effect. I kept reminding myself of how much trouble they'd all gone to.' He shook his head in mock disbelief, 'I must be going soft in my old age!'

'Well, there was rather an inferno blazing on top of that cake, wasn't there?' Robyn teased. 'I'm surprised you had enough puff!'

'If you don't watch it, madam,' he teased, lifting the plate and glasses out of reach, 'there will be no birthday cake and no champagne!'

She was in seventh heaven. It was all right! They strolled outside again and he led her to a relatively quiet spot and they drank and shared the cake between them.

He's choosing to spend time with me, she thought happily. I'm not just an irritation, dumped on him through circumstance; he really is doing this because he wants to.

'What are you thinking?' His voice was low, and she glanced up and saw that he was watching her with a strange kind of intensity.

'Nothing really,' she murmured, wiping any crumbs away from the edges of her carefully painted mouth, 'just thinking that this is nice, that we haven't argued for the past half an hour or so.'

'Got to be a record,' he agreed. 'How long do you think it will last?'

She smiled and shrugged, gazing away into the distance. 'Who knows?' she replied with careful neutrality. 'Five, maybe ten minutes more.'

'Well, we'd better make the most of it, then, hadn't we?' he said softly. 'Come on!' He pulled her to her feet.

'Where are we going?' she asked, gasping as he dragged her towards the barn.

'To dance!' he called behind. 'Quick! Before this record finishes.'

Space in the large living-room was at a premium; it was hot and dark and full of couples moving and jiving, and it was just wonderful. It was an old number, fast and furious, and he held her hand and twirled her around, pulling her in close, propelling her away, looking relaxed and so unlike the Luke Denner that she had come to love to hate that she wondered if she wasn't hallucinating.

What does it matter? she thought, as Luke scooped her into his arms and moved her round the room. It's happening, we're not fighting, just enjoy it, Robyn— while it lasts!

The record came to an end and everyone clapped and gave high-spirited whoops and whistles. 'Still want them to go home in one hour?' Robyn half shouted through the noise.

He smiled and nodded, pulling her into his arms, so that he could speak close to her ear. 'You bet! I'm far too old to keep this sort of pace going. I need a slow, sedentary number now, just so that I can get my breath back.'

Just as Luke had finished speaking, the slowest, smoochiest record began to play.

'Well, well,' he murmured, softly, 'I couldn't have worked that more smoothly even if I'd tried, could I?'

Robyn felt the heat of his body as his arms pulled her towards him. He held her close, one hand at her waist, the other supporting her back, his fingers stroking at the base of her neck, sending delightful shivers, signals of desire, up and down her spine.

Dancing had never been like this. Robyn closed her eyes, leaning her face against his shirt, and felt the thud of his heart beneath the fabric, smelt the clean, fresh maleness of his body. She wanted the record to last forever, because somehow she couldn't believe that this incredible moment would ever be repeated again—surely she would never feel such anticipation, such sharp, glorious pleasure. It wouldn't last—nothing as wonderful as this ever did; common sense told her their truce was just a transitory thing, things between them were too volatile, too unstable. She had to convince herself that if she allowed her feelings for just one second to soar away untethered she'd be doomed. Doomed to disappointment.

'So how old are you?' Robyn pulled away from his body a little and looked into his eyes. She smiled. 'Or is that information classified?'

'It should be,' he murmured, 'but with Melissa around I've got no chance.'

'You've known her a long while?' Robyn asked with careful lightness.

Luke smiled. 'Feels like an eternity, but no, not that long. Paul married her about four years ago. It was a whirlwind affair; I don't think Paul knows to this day what hit him.' He gave a wry smile. 'But then you've met her; you know what I mean.' He stroked a strand of hair from her face, and Robyn forced herself not to shiver with delight at the gentleness of his touch. 'Paul says she keeps him young.'

'There's quite an age-difference, then?' Robyn asked as he pulled her close to him once again.

'Mmm, fifteen years or so—too much anyway.'

'You think so?' Robyn felt a sudden anxiety, although she absolutely refused to admit its cause, or acknowledge the relief she felt when she realised there were only ten years between herself and Luke.

'I know so,' Luke replied. 'I hate to say it, but their marriage doesn't have a hope in hell.'

'Simply because of their ages? I can't believe that,' Robyn replied. 'Surely age doesn't matter, not when you love someone.'

'Ah, well, love—now that's an elusive emotion,' he said levelly. 'Don't tell me Robyn Drew actually believes love conquers all!'

Yes, Robyn thought, I do, I do. But he was teasing, so instead she said lightly, 'I always was a sucker for a good fairy tale.'

'Me too!' He gave a predatory smile. 'I tell you what—you be beauty and I'll be the beast!' And then he pulled her in close again and ravaged her neck so that Robyn shrieked aloud and knew all the while that she was falling deeper and deeper. . .

'Another drink?' He kept hold of her hand once the music had ended and lead her over to the french windows. 'Or something to eat?'

Robyn smiled. 'I'd like a long, cold drink, please,' she murmured, 'something really refreshing.'

His mouth twisted into a devastating smile, and he pulled her outside into the warm evening sunshine. Robyn saw the sexy curve of his mouth, the sparkle in his eyes and felt her body automatically respond.

'You know I'm going to have to kiss you first,' he murmured seductively, dragging her close to his body.

'Kiss. . .' Robyn repeated in a quivering voice. But before she could finish his mouth had covered hers and she had no time to analyse the consequences or curse herself for being so weak.

His mouth was warm and firm, hungry, moving against hers with complete command so that when he lifted his head and looked down at her with glittering eyes she was breathless.

Robyn swallowed and tried in vain to look at least mildly composed. She leant back against the wall of the barn for support, feeling the roughness of the stone against her bare shoulders, watching him, knowing the message in his gaze, that look that told her his kiss could be just the beginning.

'Now your drink,' he murmured with a wicked gleam in his eyes, 'although anything else and I'll have to consider.'

'So if I'm hungry, then?' Robyn enquired with mock innocence. 'Another kiss?'

'You've got it.' He moved his palm along the curve of her shoulder and she shivered with delight as the rough, calloused hand scorched her skin. 'Are you hungry by any chance?'

Robyn let out a short breath. 'Starving,' she murmured, meeting his intense gaze, knowing her words were dangerous, exciting, heavy with sensuous meaning. 'But I lose my appetite when there are crowds around.' He moved his mouth to her neck and she felt his tongue tantalising her skin. 'They'll be going soon, Robyn,' 'Will you wait, so that we can enjoy a good, long, slow meal together?'

She wanted to melt against him, become absorbed by him. The strength of her need was at a peak, heightened somehow because of the noise and the crowd all around them. They were ensconced, it seemed to Robyn, in their own private world, oblivious of anything except the desire that was building between them. She struggled to keep a hold of her emotions, but his mouth was having the most detrimental effect on her senses. Things were moving so fast; she needed time, a moment's respite from the onslaught of such wonderful sensations.

'. . . I think I better go and get my. . .my handbag,' she managed at last. 'I left it in the jeep.'

He kissed her lips one more time. 'Fine,' he replied, 'but don't leave it too long. In exactly——' he glanced at his wristwatch and gave a slow, sexy smile '—twenty-seven minutes this lot are getting kicked out. I said one hour, and one hour is all they're going to get.' He gave her a meaningful look. 'I've only got so much will-power.'

Twenty-seven minutes. Robyn let out a deep breath as she strolled up the dusty track, forcing her inflamed body to relax in the last vestiges of evening sun. She wanted him so much, longed to feel more than simply his mouth on hers. If they had been alone. . . She shook her head in disbelief; everything was suddenly moving at breakneck speed. This visit, like the last, had taken her totally by surprise.

If she wasn't careful, things would move too fast.

But that's what I want, she thought; I'm ready. I've been feeling so wretched these past two weeks because we've been apart. God knows, I must be masochistic or something. But my life's been empty without him, without that uncompromising presence. Now we're together, I want things to happen. More than anything, I want Luke to make love to me again.

CHAPTER NINE

ROBYN climbed into the jeep, picked up her handbag from the passenger seat and tipped it upside-down, emptying out the disgraceful collection of junk into her lap. She had bought a new handbag this morning, a neat, compact little thing that matched perfectly with the new dress and shoes she was wearing. A quick change-over of the contents, attention to her make-up and she could be back at the barn with Luke in under five minutes.

She rummaged through the assorted pile, looking for her new lipstick and perfume, and spotted the mail which she had collected from the postman first thing, on her way to the shops. There was quite a bundle. She flicked through swiftly, hunting for a comb at the same time. Nothing but bills as usual—she didn't seem to get a great deal else these days. But no, wait a minute; at the bottom there was a handwritten letter.

She opened the thick blue envelope, vaguely intrigued by its northern postmark, and scanned its contents quickly, her mind with Luke at the barn. She wouldn't rush back—that might imply she couldn't wait to be with him again—but on the other hand she didn't want to leave it too long; there were plenty of women, Melissa included, she had noticed, who had had their limpet-like eyes firmly glued to his face. Things were going so well that she didn't want anyone else interfering with what she had worked so hard for. And what is that? The small voice inside asked. What exactly are you rushing back for? The job's been won, there is no need to hang around, you've proved the point—that was all that you wanted to do in the beginning, wasn't it?

She ignored the voice and the other worry tugging at her mind—the knowledge that his need for her was a purely sexual one. He found her attractive; all her efforts had not been in vain, there was no mistaking the sensuous gleam in his eyes, the predatory twist of his smile that told Robyn exactly how he'd like the evening to end. I still want him, she thought; I still want him to take me in his arms, hold me, love me. . .

She unfolded the page of blue paper and focused on the letter instead, hardly understanding it at first reading. What was this man—she glanced down to the bottom of the page, to where his signature was scrawled—this man Charles Austin going on about? She went through again more carefully this time, and felt the instant lurch of dismay, as the gist of the letter finally sank in.

He was a friend of Mark's—an actor friend, who had been working on the same film as Mark when he had died. She re-read his covering note again, picking up and turning over the other enclosed letter in her hands. Mark's last letter, crumpled now, a little grubby. He had asked Charles to post it for him, given it to him just hours before his fatal car drive. . .Charles had written:

Sorry, but I mislaid it, and then what with the shock of Mark's accident. . . I feel you should have it. . .

Robyn gazed at the envelope, tracing the oh, so familiar illegible scrawl that was Mark's writing with trembling fingers. She knew she would open it, but when she did it would be as if he were with her all over again, and she would suffer so. . .

Why had he written a letter anyway? she wondered thoughtfully. Postcards, zany and ridiculously silly, had been more his style—she had a whole collection of them stashed away somewhere. One day she would bring them out to read and recollect. One day.

She took a deep breath and ripped the envelope open swiftly—— Well, there was only one way to find out.

The first line made her wince, it was so totally Mark.

Hi, Robyn,
Don't faint with shock, but I felt like writing you a letter! How are you, beautiful sister?

Robyn closed her eyes for a second, took a breath and then continued reading. Mark's offbeat description of the beautiful French countryside, the heat, the food, was as entertaining as always and then his style changed and the real reason for writing became evident.

> This God-damn film! It was supposed to be my big break, do you remember? But it's not going too well for me, Robyn. Hell! That's the biggest understatement of all time! The role is demanding and the director's such an arrogant bastard! Nothing I seem to do is right. I'm in hot water over various things— nothing important enough to bore you with, but I know the director wants shot of me—he's said as much and I'm sure my days are numbered; I feel like I'm struggling to keep my head above water— Oh, I know this particular pool was going to be deep, but he's there waiting just above the surface to shove me under, finding some half-baked reason to be rid of me. I know I've been a bit stupid, but I'm trying to get my act together and all Luke-do-it-all-Denner does is give me a hard time! Damn that man! He's got to be the meanest son of a bitch I've ever had the misfortune to work for. . .

Robyn pressed her hand to her mouth, read his words two—three times, staring down at Mark's writing to where that name was etched indelibly in black ink, and felt as if the anguish had paralysed every part of her.

She stared ahead through the windscreen with unseeing eyes. It couldn't be true, could it? Luke had been the director on that film? No, surely not! She shook her head, as if by the strength of her will she could make it all untrue. Coincidence couldn't be so cruel, so twisted, could it? Robyn sat staring into space, her mind numb with shock and disbelief, total agonising disbelief. She stared at the letter again, thinking hard, despairing. But why shouldn't it be true? she reasoned. He was a film director, he had told her so himself, and Mark was— had been—an actor. . .

Sickness rose, vying with the pain, as she found herself piecing together the last few hours of Mark's life. He had been driving along the twisting moutain roads when he'd crashed; that much she knew. Now her vivid imagination had no difficulty in showing her how Mark's last drive alone must have been, how miserable he must have felt. He had been driving too fast, that was what the police had said, and she could believe it now—he always had, when he was down, sunk into that deep trough of depression that occasionally consumed him, so that he lost all self-belief, all self-esteem.

And it had been Luke's fault. Robyn's eyes hardened as she remembered Mark's words. He had made Mark's life a misery, been instrumental in his death.

She swallowed and fought against the tears. 'I'm so sorry, Mark,' she whispered, 'so sorry.'

She took a deep breath and tried to think what she should do. There was a terrible urge within her to just run away and hide, curl up into a tiny ball and forget that she had made such a stupid, stupid mistake by allowing herself to fall in love with someone as ruthless and cold as Luke Denner.

There! she thought, with a terrible ache of her heart, I've finally admitted it! How ironic that it should take me so long to know how I feel about a man and then in that same moment realise that he really is the bastard I first took him for!

But I don't love him! she told herself desperately. I can't! It's not real. . . He killed Mark. . .he killed Mark. . .

She was breathing heavily, as if just the strain of knowing was wearing her out, exhausting her physically. Could she face Luke now? Confront him with everything? Tell him exactly what she thought of his cold, callous treatment of Mark?

Robyn bit her lip, hesitating. I must be strong, for Mark's sake, she thought; I owe him that much at the very least.

She wanted to cry—no, not just cry, sob and wail and beat her hands in uncontrolled anger on the steering-wheel. It can't be, she wanted to wail aloud, it just can't be!

Robyn Drew wanted to run away, but she wasn't going to. With a sudden violent movement she stuffed the letters into the glove compartment on the dashboard. She got down from the jeep, straightened her dress and headed back towards the barn.

If it was the last thing she ever did, she would make sure that Luke Denner knew exactly what she thought of him.

'Why don't you just turn around, get back in that pathetic jeep of yours and go home?'

I don't need this! Robyn thought wearily, not now.

She had been walking back along the track, head bent, deep in thought. At the sound of Melissa's strident tones she pulled up sharply and saw that her second least favourite person was standing squarely in front of her, thin arms folded determinedly across a rather too revealing cleavage.

'Something upsetting you?' Robyn asked evenly.

'No one's invited you to this party!' Melissa replied harshly. 'I organised this little surprise for Luke—it's for friends only, so I suggest you do as I say and turn around now.'

'Luke asked me to stay,' Robyn informed her flatly, trying to side-step around her. 'Why don't you see him if you're not happy about my presence?'

'It won't get you anywhere, you know——' Melissa moved remarkably swiftly, blocking her path '—hanging around Luke the way you do, finding excuses so that you can conveniently stay the weekend. He's had plenty of dealing with your sort—he's not fooled for one minute and neither am I!'

Robyn narrowed her eyes and found that the depth of dislike she felt for this hard-faced, over-made-up woman was plunging to a new-found low. 'My sort?' she queried carefully. 'What exactly do you mean by that?'

'Gold-digger!' Melissa spat out the word derisively and with quite an excessive amount of venom. 'You've had your eye on the main chance from the very beginning, haven't you? Luke's an influential and powerful man—the film industry always has been a glamorous lure for young, hopeful girls—and he's wealthy too. If you suppose. . .'

Robyn saw for the first time that Melissa was a little

drunk; her eyes had that bright, fixed look, and her words were pronounced with the extra care of someone who had consumed rather too much alcohol. 'Do yourself a favour, Melissa, and keep that over-painted mouth of yours shut!' she snapped, suddenly losing all patience. 'What's the matter?' she asked with swift acidity, as Melissa's mouth sagged for a fraction of a second because of the unexpected ferocity of her reply. 'Hasn't Luke asked you to dance this evening?'

Melissa recovered. 'You're just a little tart!' she spat out viciously. 'Do you really think Luke would be interested in someone like you? He needs someone with style, taste, experience.'

'Like you, do you mean?' Robyn asked coolly, aware that this was in danger of turning into a real humdinger of a slanging match—if it hadn't achieved that status already! 'Look, I realise you've got a fixation about Luke,' she continued swiftly, 'but don't take it out on me! It's hardly my fault, is it, if Luke hasn't noticed you exist as a woman?'

Melissa's eyes glinted murder and Robyn knew she had hit the mark. For a split second she honestly thought Melissa was going to slap her face. Then, amazingly the witchlike expression changed and her eyes lit up and a serene smile replaced the twisted hard lines of her mouth.

Luke was approaching.

Robyn forced a deep, controlled breath and arranged her own face into an expression of neutrality.

'Well, well! Nice to see you two getting to know one another!'

He had to be joking! Robyn turned, forcing herself to ignore the sudden uncontrollable lurch in the pit of her stomach, the slight tremble in her hands that would surely take a hold if she let it. She looked for sarcasm in his expression and spotted it, just for an instant, hidden in the slight curve at the corner of his mouth.

He came over and stood beside Melissa and smiled with infuriating cheerfulness. 'So, what were you two talking so animatedly about?'

Robyn glanced at Melissa's butter-wouldn't-melt-in-mouth expression.

'Melissa. . .' she hesitated and decided to go ahead '. . .was just pointing out that I hadn't been invited to your birthday party.'

'Were you?' Luke looked down at her and gave her a grim look. 'Not very sociable of you, Melissa, was it?'

She turned noticeably paler under her layers of Mediterranean tan, and tried to look quite innocent—which, Robyn thought drily, must be incredibly difficult. 'Oh, no, Luke, Robyn must have misunderstood me. Of course I wouldn't say anything——'

'Paul's inside,' Luke announced pointedly, cutting her dead. 'I know he's been looking for you. Why don't you go and give him a surprise, actually pay your husband some attention for once, eh?'

His tone brooked no argument. Melissa flushed vivid puce, threw him a look that would have had weaker men quailing, and stormed off.

'Being reminded that she's actually married always comes as rather a blow,' Luke commented, watching her go.

'You knew she was lying?' Robyn enquired coldly.

'It stands out a mile; she never was much of an actress,' he drawled. 'Your comment over dinner that evening, about her acting in cheap soap operas, was quite apt; I don't think she's ever forgiven you for that.' He turned and curved amused, sensuous lips at Robyn. 'You hit the mark—the big time, despite a thousand auditions, has always eluded her.' His eyes narrowed suddenly, scanning her face. 'Hey, what's up?' he asked, tilting her chin with one long finger so that Robyn found her face raised to his, with no option but to look right into his piercing eyes. 'Did she give you a hard time?'

Robyn turned away sharply, glancing down at the dusty ground at her feet. 'Oh, she called me a tart, a gold-digger, nothing I couldn't handle,' she murmured.

'She did what?' He looked incredulous and then fiercely angry. 'That woman!' he snarled, glaring back at the barn. 'Wait till I get my hands on her! Look,' he added, taking hold of Robyn's arm, 'if ever she starts on

you like that again, just bring me into it—I'll sort her
out.'

Robyn stepped away violently, shrugging off his hold.
'I don't need you to fight my battles for me!' she flared.
'I can look after myself!'

'Hey! Don't take it out on me, Robyn,' he replied.
'Melissa's upset you, I can see that, but I'm not to
blame.'

'Oh, come on!' Robyn said with mocking sweetness.
'You don't think I'm that naïve, do you? She's as
frustrated as hell, besotted by you! What's the matter?
Haven't you taken her to bed recently?'

The cool blue of his eyes glinted ice. 'For your
information—not that it's any of your damned business,
of course,' he replied quietly, 'but I have never, nor will
I ever, go to bed with Melissa.'

'No?' Robyn's smile revealed derisive disbelief.

'Are you looking for a fight, lady?' he demanded
tersely. 'Because if you are you're sure as hell going the
right way to getting one! Paul happens to be a very good
friend and I don't believe in doing the dirty on my
friends, OK?' He thrust his face close to hers suddenly
and made her jump, pulling her round so that she was
close and more aware of his dominant masculinity.

Robyn trembled, forcing herself to stand her ground.
'Scruples?' She managed somehow to raise her eyebrows
in mock surprise. 'In the cut and thrust of the film
world?' she queried bitterly. 'I thought morals and
loyalty were laughable attributes. Doesn't everyone just
take what they want and damn the consequences?'

'No, they don't!' he snapped. 'Why should they? It's
a profession, just like any other. Most of us are in it
because we love what we do, because we want to
contribute something. We work our way in and, if we're
any good, we work our way up. Believe it or not, but we
do not tread all over each other to get where we want to
go—or at least the majority of us don't!'

Robyn thought of Mark, the film last year. 'And when
things go wrong?' she enquired sharply. 'What happens
then?'

He shrugged, releasing her. 'It's inconvenient, frustrating, but you do your best—mostly things turn out well in the end.'

What about Mark? she wanted to scream. Was his death just an inconvenience? She turned from him, not able to control her expression any longer. It was exhausting. She couldn't go through with it. But after a hesitant pause she found herself saying, 'I believe you had a slight mishap on a film last year—in France. That must have been very irritating for you.'

There was a pause. 'You mean the actor who died? How did you hear about that?' he asked sharply.

Robyn closed her eyes and swallowed and dug her nails deep into her palms. 'Oh, from Melissa; she mentioned something about it,' she said vaguely, 'Y. . .you were the director on that film?' It was her last clutch at hope—her final chance that somehow Mark had made a mistake, hallucinated. . .anything.

'Yes, that's right.' His tone gave little away. If she could find the courage to turn and look at him, she might read some clue into his expression. Tell me, then! she urged silently, when he allowed the silence to fall between them. Tell me about Mark! Help me to understand! But he wasn't going to.

When she finally spun around, she saw that he was striding around the side of the barn to the kitchen.

This wasn't how she had planned it—not that she had really planned anything, but she had pictured herself, cold and ferocious, confronting him, shocking him with the knowledge that he had virtually killed her brother. She took a deep breath and then hastened after him; it was cowardly but she was deserate for something, some insight, some new aspect that would save her from having to hate him.

'It was a car accident, wasn't it?' Her voice was breathless, partly from exertion, mostly from the sheer tension and strain of talking about it. She pushed her way through a high-spirited crowd who didn't seem to notice her rudeness and followed him into the kitchen.

'Why the interest?' He grabbed the nearest bottle of

whisky and poured a measure into a glass, watching her over the rim.

'I. . . I just. . .' She struggled to think of some plausible reason, to raise her voice above the incessant beat of the music, which was so loud, despite the closed door. 'I'm just interested, that's all.' It sounded ridiculously lame and she cursed herself for sounding so weak and ineffectual, but miraculously he seemed not to notice.

'He was driving too fast. If you weren't familiar with them, the roads up in the moutains were treacherous. It was a complete and utter waste of life.' His voice was flat, unemotional—bored even? She watched him tilt back his head and swallow most of the amber-coloured liquid in one large draught.

'Was he a. . .a good actor?' Her mouth had formed the words before she realised. It was as painful as hell, and she despised herself for even caring what he had thought of Mark's abilities, but for some reason she desperately needed to know.

'I believed so originally, when I first cast him,' he replied briskly, piercing her with his ice-blue gaze. 'Unfortunately he never actually produced any of his potential on the set. In fact,' he added, with more than a hint of irritation in his voice, 'he turned out to be quite a disruptive influence.'

'Rather a blessing in disguise, then—his death,' Robyn snapped shakily. 'Life must have been easier once he had gone!'

He threw her a disbelieving look. 'God, Robyn! What the hell's got into you? You don't honestly expect me to agree to a statement like that, do you?' he snapped violently. 'What the hell do you take me for? A complete bastard? The man died, for heaven's sake!'

'Who died?' Callum came in just then, whistling to the music, apparently oblivious to the air of angry tension, the sparks that emanated dangerously between Luke and Robyn. He staggered a little, or perhaps it was a weird sort of dance, and then rooted around among the half-empty plates, cramming whatever food he could find into his mouth.

'Get lost, Callum!' Luke's voice was terse. He didn't even bother to look at him.

Callum gave a slightly nervous laugh and glanced towards Robyn.

'Didn't you hear what I said?' Luke said savagely, turning to glare at Callum, who continued to pile food on to a plate.

'You were joking weren't you?' the blond man asked, smiling warily at Luke.

'No, I damn well wasn't!' Luke replied bluntly. 'So get out.'

'Well, pardon me for breathing!' Callum muttered, as he retreated back towards the door.

'Wait for me, Callum!' Robyn called hastily, throwing Luke a disgusted glare. 'I'd like that dance you asked for earlier.' Had he? She couldn't remember; neither, it seemed, could Callum. He looked momentarily surprised and then, after throwing Luke a somewhat triumphant look, he smiled and took her by the hand, and led her through into the living-room.

Callum held her close in the darkened room and she smelt the slightly sour smell of beer on his breath, felt the too intimate touch of his hands on her body as they moved in a slow circle around and among the tightly packed bodies.

What am I doing? she thought despondently. Why on earth didn't I just tell Luke everything and get the hell out? I pushed myself through the agony of broaching the subject of Mark's death and then, when I had the opportunity to finish the deed and expose the truth of my association, tell Luke what a low-down swine he is, I crumbled like a coward.

'This is nice,' Callum murmured in her ear, 'very nice. You're a great mover, Robyn. Shall we dance some more?' he asked as the record finally came to an end.

Robyn pulled away from his grasp. 'No, I don't think so,' she replied, beating a hasty retreat to the edge of the room. 'I'm feeling a bit thirsty.'

She had no intention of dancing another record with him; Callum's hands were far too slippery—in fact she was beginning to regret having anything to do with him at all; the pleasant, confident smile that had greeted her at the beginning of the evening had now turned into a quite definite leer.

She smoothed a weary hand across her eyes and then looked up and saw Luke over the far side of the room, gazing at her with impenetrable eyes. He had a woman on his arm—that girl, the model, long-legged, beautiful, glimpsed in many glossy magazines. Robyn felt the sting of his mocking expression and hurriedly averted her eyes from his face, forcing herself to turn to Callum with an animated smile.

'Do you fancy a drink?' he asked.

Robyn nodded gratefully; she was dry and hot and thirsty. 'Please—something long and cool. No alcohol, though,' she added. 'I've got to drive home.'

She watched as Callum wove his way through the various clusters of people and found her eyes irresistibly drawn to the corner where Luke stood, surrounded by a large group of his friends. She watched his rugged composure, heard his deep, distinctive laugh and felt anger swelling inside. I could go across now, she thought. I could sidle up to the hi-fi and turn it off, snap on the light-switch and announce quite calmly to all the sycophants here that Luke Denner is nothing more than a callous murderer. She tried to imagine herself doing it and then heaved a small sigh. What would she gain? Nobody would take her seriously, Luke would laugh it off and take control of the situation, belittle her in front of his friends. . .and, besides, did she really want Mark's death brought down to the level of party-stopper? No. That wasn't the way. She would regain her own composure, wait just a little longer for the right opportunity and then she would strike.

'Here you go.' Callum handed her a tall glass of orange juice, which Robyn accepted thankfully. She tilted her head back and took a long, refreshing drink.

'So is there something going on between you and Luke?' Callum asked.

She tried to look surprised. 'No, of course not,' she replied a fraction too quickly.

'The atmosphere was pretty heated when I barged

into the kitchen,' he replied, adding with a rueful grin, 'And I, like many others, saw you dancing with Luke earlier—that was pretty heated too. Or', he added, looking directly into her eyes, 'have I got it all wrong?'

He wanted to know how the land lay. Robyn found herself hesitating, but only for a fraction of a second. Out of the corner of her eye, she saw the casual intimacy as Luke bent to say something to the girl, felt the cruel, jealous twist in her body, as she saw his mouth meeting hers in a lazy kiss.

'There's nothing between Luke Denner and me, except business and an overriding sense of dislike,' she said firmly.

'Sure?' Callum asked, smiling, immediately winding an arm around her waist.

Robyn took another sip of her drink. 'Sure,' she murmured defiantly. 'As far as I'm concerned Luke Denner is just another client for my landscape business.'

'Well, I'm very pleased to hear that.' Callum pressed his body in a little closer, nuzzled his lips against the skin at her neck. 'Shall we have another dance?'

The record was slow and even smoochier than before. Robyn backed away a little and shook her head. Callum was coming on too strong. 'No, not just now,' she smiled. 'I'm feeling a bit peckish; I think I'll just go and see if there's any food left—won't be a minute.' She left him suddenly before he could argue, or offer to accompany her, and dived through the crowd towards the kitchen.

'Running away from him already?' Luke grabbed hold of her arm and brought her up short, half dragging her through, banging the kitchen door shut behind them. 'So, what new little game are you playing this time?' he snarled, glaring at her with a taut expression.

'Game?' Robyn repeated, shaken by his rough handling and sudden appearance. 'I'm not playing at any game.'

'No! And neither am I!' he growled, moving threateningly towards her, so that Robyn found herself retreating back against the wall. 'So start talking, tell me what the hell's got into you! It's clear our little truce has come to a grinding halt. One minute you're like fire in my arms, the next you're as cold as ice. Can't you handle it—is that the problem?'

He had manoeuvred her just right, pressing her into the tightest corner, standing squarely in front of her so that she had no choice but to stare into his dark, angry face.

'Nothing's got into me!' Robyn ground out, forcing herself to hold on to what little composure she had left. 'What's the matter?' she added with risky mock sweetness. 'Can't *you* handle the fact that I prefer Callum's company to yours?'

He gave a short, harsh laugh and thrust his face close. 'Callum's a creep, Robyn! You know it and so do I. So don't waste your breath! I saw the way you had to fight him off in that first dance—the bastard's hands were everywhere!'

'And yours weren't earlier, I suppose?' Robyn enquired with as much derisive sarcasm as she could muster, deliberately blocking out the memory of how wonderful it had felt with Luke and how sordid and somehow dirty it had felt when Callum had touched her. 'You're just seeing what you want to see!' she retorted. 'Callum's an attractive man; why shouldn't I enjoy his company?'

'OK, then, tell me!' he demanded forcibly. 'Tell me you enjoy Callum's company rather than mine.'

His body was touching hers, the hard length of his thighs pressing against her own. She could feel the warmth of his breath, knew the savage lips were threatening a kiss, promising. . .

Robyn swallowed and struggled to keep the anger she felt at the forefront of her mind. But when he was near, like this. . .

'I prefer Callum's company to yours,' she whispered, challenging him with her eyes, 'any day!'

He lowered his mouth then and brushed his lips against hers, so that Robyn surprised by the gentleness that was so at odds with his temper, found herself momentarily confused. 'Repeat it!' he commanded huskily against the softness of her mouth. 'Only make it sound as if you really believe it this time.'

'Stop it!' Robyn whispered shakily. 'Let. . .let me go.'

'No way!' He took her mouth again, but this time his mouth punished her with sudden erotic savagery and she felt the treacherous swift ache of desire, the longing for more, for all of him, deep in the pit of her stomach.

'No, damn you!' she spat, finding the will-power from somewhere to drag her mouth free. 'You think that's all it takes?' She pushed against his arms in an attempt at escape, hating herself in that moment as much as him, for the way her body so easily betrayed her. Her and Mark. Poor Mark. If she admitted it, guilt had played a part in her grief. He could be wild and crazy at times and she hadn't faced up to the fact that the way he lived his life was doing him no good, no good at all. If she had only tried to make him see. . . And now, now she had even more reason to feel guilt, heavy and unbearable, pressing down, hanging around her shoulders.

She saw the mocking smile, lunged away from him and almost fell flat on her face, stumbling against a chair.

'You OK?' he enquired lazily, holding her arm, helping her to steady herself.

'What would you care?' Robyn snapped, whipping away from his hold, glaring furiously across at him. 'All you're ever bothered about is yourself, that incredible ego of yours!'

His expression changed, his eyes flashed ice-blue. 'Well, this ego, incredible or otherwise, is warning you to stay away from Callum,' he growled. 'Do as I say, Robyn, or you may find yourself in a whole load of trouble.'

'Don't threaten me, damn you!' Robyn snapped shakily. 'I'll do as I please.' She moved to the door, opened it and was about to bang it violently behind her when Luke caught hold of her again.

'I mean it, Robyn,' he said softly. 'For once in your life take some sound advice; stay away from Callum—he's only after one thing.'

She looked into his face, saw the serious expression

and gave a short, harsh laugh, fighting to hide the hurt.
'And you're not, I suppose?' she retorted harshly.

He tightened his grip and she felt the sudden fierce
strength of his fingers biting deep into her wrist. 'Don't
kid yourself!' he snarled. 'What do I need with a
childish, fickle tease like you? Go to Callum if that's
what you really want. Just don't let it be said that I
didn't warn you, that's all.'

She felt sick. Robyn pushed through the stuffy, claustrophobic room, weaving her way with difficulty through
the couples who always seem to be dancing, always
clinging together. The hot sting of tears pricked painfully at her eyes as the agony of hating him and yet
wanting him so desperately all at the same time overwhelmed her. Suddenly the only thing that mattered
was to be home, safe, away from all this noise, this heat,
the perpetual anguish.

I'm going, she thought. I'm a pathetic coward, but I
just can't go through with this. What on earth made me
imagine for even one second that I would have enough
strength to confront Luke? She took a deep, steadying
breath and tried not to picture the way he had looked,
hear the scathing tone of his voice.

She climbed the spiral staircase. She would write,
when she was away from here, tell him in no uncertain
terms exactly what she thought of him. It was a coward's
way out, of course, but the best she would ever be able
to do. At least he would know then about Mark, realise
that at least one person in this world knew him for what
he really was.

Robyn clutched the cast-iron railing and wondered
for the first time why her legs felt so shaky and weird,
why her stomach was churning so violently. If she didn't
know any better, she would have said she'd had too
much to drink, but apart from that first glass of punch,
which she'd never finished, and then Luke's celebratory
champagne, she hadn't touched alcohol all evening.

She went into the bathroom along the landing and
splashed her face with cool water. Her head was aching
a bit too, but then that was not surprising perhaps after
what she'd been through this evening.

She came to the spare bedroom, the one she had spent that first unforgettable night in, and slipped inside. The bedside cabinet held a bottle of aspirin; they might help. If she took a couple now, she'd feel better for the long drive home.

Robyn sat on the bed and tipped two tablets into the palm of her hand, resisting the need to lay her head down on the cool pillow. I must go, she thought, I must go now. But instead she sat, staring into space, transfixed with a sudden heavy tiredness, half listening to the steady, rhythmic beat of the music down below, wondering about Luke, remembering Mark.

Then she heard the click of the door and she turned, acknowledged the sudden lurch in the pit of her stomach, a half-hope that somehow there would be something he could say that would make things all right.

But it wasn't Luke, only Callum.

Robyn let out a deep breath. 'Oh, Callum,' she murmured, feeling foolish. She screwed the lid back on to the bottle and replaced it back in the cabinet.

He came over and sat close beside her on the bed, 'I've been looking for you everywhere, Robyn.'

'Have you?' Robyn gave a brief smile. 'I haven't been feeling too good; I came in here to. . .'

His hand had slid to her thigh, and she felt the lurch of dismay as his fingers slid over the silky fabric of her dress. 'Callum!' Robyn placed her hand over his, lifting it away, realising swiftly that he was more than a little drunk. 'I came up here for some headache tablets,' she continued matter-of-factly. 'I'm taking these and then I'm going to drive home.'

'Oh, come on, Robyn! Don't be such a spoil-sport!' He was slurring a little, slipping an arm along her shoulders, drawing her close into his body with a swift, clumsy movement. 'The party's only just got going and it's quiet up here, peaceful. Loosen up a little, Robyn. We could have some fun.'

'I told you I don't feel good. Fun's the last thing I feel like!' she replied swiftly, trying to pull away from the deceptive strength of his hold. 'Would you let me go, please, Callum?'

He didn't seem to hear, or rather he chose not to. He smiled down at her in a drunken, rather disquieting sort of way. 'I made a mistake, didn't I?' he murmured. 'Vodka obviously doesn't agree with you.'

Robyn's glance was sharp. 'Vodka?' she repeated. 'What do you mean?' He raised fair eyebrows and attempted a look of innocence. 'Vodka and orange juice—that's what you asked for, wasn't it? A large one, but perhaps not as large as I gave.' He grinned. 'My hand slipped. Naughty of me, wasn't it?'

Robyn pursed her lips angrily. 'That's not very funny! You know very well I said no alcohol! Look, stop this stupidness, Callum,' Robyn added irritably as he began nuzzling her neck. 'Let me get up.' She tugged at his arm in annoyance but they seemed quite immovable.

'Oh, don't be boring, Robyn!' he mumbled, and then, before she could get up, do anything, he was pushing all his weight against her, pressing her back against the bed, half lying across her, holding her wrists so that she had no way of fighting him off.

This was no joke. He was really, really drunk. Robyn felt the swift surge of alarm, and panic as the heavy weight of his body descended on top of her.

'Come on, Robyn,' he muttered thickly, forcing his hard, wet mouth against her lips, 'don't play games. You've got a great body; it's a crime not to use it.'

His mouth made her cringe, his hands moulded her flesh. 'Stop this, Callum!' she managed to gasp. 'Stop it! You're drunk; you don't know what you're doing.' Surely he would see sense, she thought, surely! His hands seemed to be everywhere, sliding over her, trying to find entry to her bra, covering her neck with hateful kisses.

'Don't I?' he responded, and she saw him leer down at her, as he clutched at her. 'Come on, baby, loosen up a little. You know you want it!'

'I'll scream,' she said shakily. 'Get off me, or I swear I will!'

He leered again. 'Scream away, then, darling; I doubt if anyone will hear—the music's very loud.'

Robyn opened her mouth, but before she could put it

to the test he clamped a hot sweaty palm over her lips. 'Tut-tut, you really are a spoil-sport, aren't you? But my, what a great body—no wonder Luke's got the hots for you. What a pity he isn't in the position that I'm in, eh?' He pressed his mouth down on hers and kissed her long and hard and without any kind of finesse until Robyn felt she'd throw up if she had to endure the taste of him any longer.

And then miraculously the weight of his body was lifted and she heard with overwhelming relief the deep, harsh tones of Luke's voice. Two words, both of them not repeatable, and then the thud, as Callum's body crunched against the far wall. Robyn hastily sat up, watched with horrified fascination as Luke dragged Callum's limp body up and prepared to hit him once again.

'Don't!' Her voice rang out feebly, no competition against the noise of the music.

Luke hesitated, grasping Callum unceremoniously around the neck with one strong hand. 'He deserves it.'

'Let him go, Luke! Please!' she cried. 'You've hurt him enough as it is; can't you see the state of his face?'

She watched as Luke fought his own anger and then half threw him to the ground. 'Get out! Right out!' he snarled, as Callum struggled to get up. 'Quickly, before I change my mind and break every bone in your disgusting body!'

Callum clutched his bleeding nose and staggered away, half crawling across the carpet. Luke helped him through the door with a violent push and then slammed it after him, flicking the lock—something, Robyn realised with relief, that Callum hadn't thought to do earlier.

'Did. . .did he hurt you?' His voice was like granite as he stared down at her, grey and hard and totally unyielding.

Robyn shook her head and swallowed. 'No,' she breathed, looking away from him because she couldn't bear to see the expression in his face. 'Not really.'

'And just what the hell is that supposed to mean?' he flashed. 'Not really! Did he or not for God's sake?'

'No! No!' she half yelled, raising her face, glaring up

into his. 'He kissed me and tried to stuff his hand down my front——' her face winced at the memory of the way his hands—and mouth had felt and she saw Luke's jaw tighten in response, his eyes harden to pure ice '—but nothing more.'

Luke looked at her with uncomprehending anger. 'How the hell could you,' he asked, 'after all that I said?'

'What?' Robyn gazed up at him, her face tight with misery.

'What?' he stormed. 'Come with him to this damned bedroom! That's what! He was drunk and as sure as hell only after one thing and you let yourself——'

'Now just you hold it there!' Robyn cried, flinging herself to her feet. 'How dare you stand there. . .?' Her voice cracked a little. 'How dare you imply that I. . .that I came in here with him to. . . I was about to go home,' she continued angrily. 'I came in here to get some tablets——'

'Another headache?' Luke cut in with heavy sarcasm. 'That can't have gone down too well. . .when did you spring that one on Callum?'

She stared at him hopelessly for a fraction of a second and then she looked away as tears sprang into her eyes. 'You bastard!' she whispered.

'So I'm a bastard,' he replied with rough laughter. 'Well, what in God's name does that make that creep Callum, eh?'

'He was drunk,' Robyn whispered. 'He didn't know what he was doing.'

'And that makes it all right?' Luke prowled the room, like a caged and very angry tiger. 'I don't believe I'm hearing this!' he said with incredulity. 'You're defending him—that pathetic excuse of a man! You do know what he was after, don't you?' he enquired savagely, turning to gaze down at her. 'Or are you still so naïve as to believe that he just wanted a comforting kiss and a cuddle?'

Robyn bit her lip. 'Surely he wouldn't have. . . have——'

'Sex can be incredibly swift, Robyn,' Luke cut in with deliberate bluntness. 'A couple of thrusts and someone like Callum is more than happy!' He turned away from her. 'Or rather rape. You hadn't consented, I presume?'

Robyn knew she couldn't bare any more. Each harsh look, each savage word was like a knife twisting in her heart. He was being so unfair, so cruel! How could I have ever believed I loved him? she cried silently. How could I have believed him capable of kindness and compassion? She ran past him, and flung herself on the door, fumbling with the catch. 'Now I know,' she yelled, turning her face to his, meeting his gaze with cold, hating eyes. 'Now I know just what Mark went through. I didn't want to believe it at first,' she told him shakily, 'but I can now. You made Mark's life a misery and he died because of it.'

'Mark?' The word was like a razor, cutting through the claustrophobic tension. 'You mean Mark Dalton?'

She gazed at him and she knew her face revealed every inch of hurt and pain and anger that she felt. 'Yes,' she replied, 'Mark Dalton.' She saw the way his eyes narrowed, the uncomprehending expression on his face. 'There's no need to look at me like that, Luke,' she said unevenly. 'I'm not drunk or crazy. Last year in France—remember? That unfortunate incident, a slight inconvenient hitch in the smooth running of your life!'

'Tell me!' he commanded sharply.

'Mark Dalton.' She spoke his name again, quietly this time because now the anger was seeping away, to be replaced by misery. 'The name he used——' she swallowed and took a hasty breath, aware of his taut features, the sudden stillness of his body '——Because I believe there already was another actor somewhere on the Equity list with the surname Drew.' She pressed her lips together, glancing at him with bleak eyes, hardly seeing Luke at all through the blur of tears. 'Mark was my brother,' she declared harshly, curling her fingers around the handle, 'and you helped kill him.'

CHAPTER TEN

THE stunned silence lengthened. Luke made no move, just looked at her, his gaze one of incredulity and shock, and Robyn felt as bad as she had ever felt in her life. Telling Luke had given her no satisfaction; there was no feeling of well-being or sweet revenge, just a cold, forlorn emptiness, where once there had been hope. She turned, wrenched open the door and hurled herself down the spiral staircase, pushing blindly through the group below, tears streaming down her face.

They might have looked at her, all those swish guests with their famous names and fast cars, but she didn't care.

She ran down the track as if the hounds of death were at her heels and struggled with the door of the jeep, snatched at the steering-wheel, fumbled with the ignition.

He was following. She heard a shout and looked up. He was weaving in and out of the cars, jumping over them when they got in his way, his face hard and grim with determination.

Robyn turned the ignition over, realising he was gaining on her with remarkable speed, and the jeep roared into life. She crashed the engine into reverse gear and felt a wave of relief because the shock of her revelation had kept him inert for too long—he wouldn't catch her. He was too late.

She looked behind and concentrated on speeding backwards down the track, giving silent thanks that she had been the last to arrive. He wouldn't be able to follow, not for many, many minutes; too many cars blocked his way, parked haphazardly. He would need to find the owners from among the mêlée inside. And by then, surely, it would not be worth the trouble.

It was a miracle Robyn got home in one piece. But the roads were quiet, the jeep's engine capacity, when pushed, seemingly knew no bounds, and some kind of warped guardian angel was on her side.

Not that it mattered, she thought; the truth was that she didn't give a damn about herself. She drove to escape, not to arrive, like an automaton, gripping the wheel in a trance, hardly aware of her surroundings, the road, the car horns and headlights that blared and flashed around her. Luke. He was all she saw now. Luke—the man she had loved. She closed her eyes as the pain of knowing rose and twisted inside. She didn't want to think, to believe. Oh, God! Why had she ever opened that letter? If there had been no letter, who knew how things might have turned out?

But that would have been worse, she thought, desperately trying to produce some lining to a cloud that hung heavy and black over her. The inevitable course for them both had been clear tonight; if she had stayed they would have made love again—there had been no question about it. The tension between them, the sexual feeling, had been at such a pitch. And then how would I have felt, she asked herself as she hurled the jeep down the motorway, finding that I'd fallen again for a man as cold and hard as that—finding out when it was too late what he was really like?

Anne, sitting watching late-night television with drooping eyes, gave a jump, then a gasp of horror, when she saw Robyn. She sprang up, knocking over her coffee-cup in the process, and clutched Robyn by the shoulders.

'Robyn, quick, tell me! What's the matter? What's wrong? Did you have an accident? What?'

The questions tumbled out, one on top of another. Robyn could barely think, let alone string coherent words together to form an answer. She suddenly felt totally drained; relief at getting home again had brought about a release of all her emotions. She sobbed and sniffed and struggled incomprehensibly for several moments, fighting to control her tears.

'Robyn, for God's sake, tell me what's going on! Are you hurt? Have you had an accident? Here, have some coffee; just stop crying and tell me!'

She accepted Anne's steaming mug and managed a few sips. I'm in shock, she thought, I must be. She looked at Anne's stricken face, contorted with worry and concern, and tried desperately to pull herself together.

'Robyn,' Anne pleaded, 'tell me, he hasn't. . . I mean, you were with him, with Luke Denner? He hasn't. . .hurt you, has he?'

Robyn shook her head. 'No. No, at least not in the way you mean. . . I. . .he. . .' She let out a deep breath and struggled against the tears.

'But it is Luke?' Anne persisted. 'The reason you're so upset? Oh, Robyn you look dreadful. ' She grabbed a handful of tissues from a box on the side. 'Here, dry your eyes.'

Robyn scrubbed at her face with the tissues and took a huge breath.

'Now,' Anne commanded, 'tell me. What's happened?'

'I. . . I had a letter from Mark,' Robyn managed shakily. 'He wrote it on the day he died, gave it to a friend to post. . .' She gulped back the tears and then blurted unsteadily, 'Luke drove him to his death, made Mark's life a misery. He was so low, so miserable.' She looked up helplessly. 'Oh, Anne, what shall I do? It's too much, too much to bear.'

Anne's face struggled to comprehend. 'Robyn, I'm lost. I don't understand. Calm down and tell me properly.' She shook her head, clearly not understanding. 'Luke Denner? Mark?'

The harsh, jarring ring of the telephone stunned them both into silence. Both stared at it almost in horror for a moment, listened to the somehow insistent, angry ringing. 'That's him!' Robyn wailed. 'Don't answer it, Anne, please!'

Anne glanced at the phone worriedly, then at Robyn's ashen, panic-stricken face. 'Robyn, calm down—please! You're in danger of becoming hysterical. If it is Luke, I'll just say you're not here, OK?' She crossed the room and with a resolute shrug of her shoulders picked up the receiver. 'Of course, it's probably not him anyway,' she added.

It was.

'This is Luke Denner. I need to speak to Robyn. Is she with you?'

'Hello,' Anne replied, glancing across at Robyn who moved restlessly now around the room. 'Umm— Robyn? Well, no, I'm sorry, she's not here. . . I . . . I thought she was with you. What's the problem?'

'Hell!' There was a pause. 'Look, she was with me, I can't explain now, but I'm sure she'll be with you soon. I'm driving down now. When she arrives, keep her there. Don't let her leave, whatever you do. I must speak to her.'

He replaced the receiver abruptly and Anne turned to a tense, white-faced Robyn and repeated his side of the conversation. 'He sounded terribly fierce, Robyn,' she commented worriedly. 'Oh, what's going on? Tell me, for heaven's sake. How could Luke Denner possibly have driven Mark to his death? It's so. . .so melodramatic!'

'Anne, I can't stay here!' Robyn cried. 'Luke's coming and I don't want to see him; I couldn't bear it.' She sprang from her seat like a woman possessed. 'I can't see him! I've got to think of something, somewhere. . .' Robyn turned away, twisting her fingers distractedly.

'Robyn, calm down!' Anne implored. 'Tell me properly, what's going on? How could Luke have had anything to do with Mark's death?'

Robyn closed her eyes and made a tremendous effort. When she spoke again her voice was calm, more composed, and Anne's face took on a less worried appearance. 'Mark was miserable, Anne,' she began. 'You knew how he could get if his acting wasn't working out—it was about the only thing that could really bring him down.' She hesitated. 'Luke's a director. Did I tell you that? I can't remember; I wasn't aware of it myself in the beginning.' She paused, placed a trembling hand over her eyes. 'Mark wrote to me—a letter of all things. I suppose I should have been suspicious then, realised something wasn't right.' She smiled and gave a forced laugh. 'You remember how Mark hated writing. It was a lot if I got one jokey line from him on the back of a postcard. Anyway, he waffled on for a little while about everything that didn't matter and then. . .' she swallowed '. . .then he got down to it and told me about everything that did.'

'And?' Anne asked. 'What happened?'

'There was terrible friction between the two of them; they obviously argued badly, Mark was having problems of one sort and another, and Luke Denner. . .' she gave a harsh laugh '. . .well, he. . .he just made life hard, didn't give Mark a chance, any help. I found out tonight what he can be like when he's angry. I can imagine what he was like with Mark.' Robyn clenched the tissues into a fierce ball. 'Mark needed help—something wasn't going right. Why didn't Luke damn well help him, instead of threatening to throw him off the film? Oh, Anne,' she whispered, shaking her head, 'don't you see? I've betrayed him, betrayed my own brother.'

Anne listened quietly, her expression revealing her sympathy for Robyn. She hadn't known Mark very well, but she had been there for Robyn when he had died, seen the agony that her friend had gone through.

'Oh, Robyn, this must have been an awful shock—and you were with Luke at the time? So did he know all along, then, that you are—were,—' she corrected swiftly, 'Mark's sister? Is that what you're saying?'

'No.' Robyn looked confused. 'No, I don't know; he might have known I suppose, but I don't think so.' She shook her head, considering wildly. 'No, he couldn't have, because Mark didn't use his real surname, did he? But Anne, I'm so mixed up, confused, so unhappy.'

Anne studied Robyn for a few moments. 'Luke Denner wasn't just a client, was he?' she murmured softly. 'There was something more between the two of you; that's why this is so awful for you.' She hesitated. 'Am I right?'

'Yes. No!' Robyn shook her head, pacing the room. 'Oh, I don't know! There was something. Oh, what I told you before was quite true—we did argue all the time.He didn't have any faith in me——' she let out a breath '—but there was something else. . .an incredible feeling. . .an electricity. Oh, of course it was just sexual on his part.' Robyn gazed across at Anne. 'I don't think there's much doubt that as a person I ranked pretty low, but for me——' she shook her head '—well, I've just never felt so attracted, so compelled by someone, the way I did with him. He managed somehow to get under my skin, tangle me up inside so that I didn't know if I was coming or going. He maddened me, yet I couldn't wait to be with him.'

She paused and her voice fell to a half-whisper. 'We made love.' She saw Anne's expression and gave a harsh, bitter laugh. 'I know, stupid of me, wasn't it? Naïve, that's what he was always calling me—that or juvenile, and you can't get more juvenile or naïve than allowing a man like Luke Denner to seduce you and then half hoping, almost believing in the fantasy that somehow you might actually mean something to him!'

Robyn pressed her lips together and half turned so that Anne wouldn't see the tears that were welling up in her eyes again. 'I think the moment when I really fell completely overboard was the night of my dream,' she continued, half talking to herself. 'It was the usual one—the one where I'm searching for Mark. I made a real fool of myself, crying and sobbing, but Luke held me and comforted me and he was so kind. . .' She shook her head in disbelief at the memory. 'Just shows you what a pathetic judge of character I am, doesn't it?' she added bitterly.

'Do you love him?' Anne asked gently. 'Is that what you're saying?'

'How can I?' Robyn's voice held venom suddenly. 'How can I honestly feel that way, knowing what he did to Mark—the way he treated him?'

Anne sat on the settee and hugged her legs beneath her. 'But do you really know everything?' she asked, in a quiet voice.

'What do you mean?' Robyn looked puzzled suddenly.

'You read Mark's letter, felt for him, saw his side, which is entirely understandable, but did you give Luke a chance to explain, tell you how it was for him?'

'No!' Robyn replied tautly, 'I didn't. Look, don't do this to me, Anne,' she added, seeing the expression of

surprise on her friend's face. 'Mark was my brother; I
know he had his faults, but he was never a liar.'

'Oh, that's not what I'm saying!' Anne said swiftly.
'You know that! But Mark was down; he wrote to you
and told you how it was from his point of view, with his
perspective. You're seeing this from just one side.'

Robyn turned and looked away, reliving the last awful
moments with Luke. How could Anne understand? She
only knew a fraction of how it had been. 'I won't see
him, Anne,' she said fiercely. 'I won't! I hate Luke
Denner for what he's done.'

Anne raised her hands in a placatory gesture and
came across to give her a comforting hug. 'OK. Take it
easy,' she murmured soothingly. 'You're upset. You
need space, time to think, I can see that. This has come
as a terrible shock. It's not surprising you feel as you do.
When Luke arrives, we won't let him in. He'll just have
to drive all the way back home.'

Robyn shook her head. 'You still don't understand, do
you, Anne?' she said earnestly. 'Because you've never
met Luke. He's so determined, so forceful—he does
what he wants and to hell with the consequences! There's
no way he'll be deterred by you or a closed front door!'

Anne look sceptical. 'Oh, come on! Aren't you simply
being alarmist? What are you saying—that he'll enter
here by force?'

'Anne, I'm not. I wish I were, and yes, he probably will
do if he doesn't get his own way. He's like that. You
heard for yourself how he sounded on the phone; he said
he'll be down. It's quite a drive—I've just gone through
it myself; doesn't that indicate to you how serious he is?'

'Well, he did sound sort of forceful, I'll give you that,'
Anne conceded slowly. 'So what are you going to do?'
she added worriedly, after a moment's hesitation.

'I'm going away,' Robyn replied, walking through to
her bedroom. 'Somewhere. To a hotel, a quiet place
where he won't find me. I'll get some things together
and think, decide as I go along. All I know is I can't stay
here—I can't handle seeing him.'

Anne followed her through and watched as Robyn
stuffed clothes frantically into an overnight bag. 'But

Robyn, it's almost midnight! There's nowhere at this time of night!'

Robyn bit her lip. 'There must be! I've got to have some time alone. Time to sort myself out. If need be, I'll just drive myself around and then find somewhere in the morning.'

'Well, if you're serious about all this,' Anne murmured after a hesitant pause, 'there is my cottage in Wales.'

Robyn spun round, her face bright for a moment with relief. 'Oh, Anne! Yes, of course! Can I go there? Would it be all right?'

Anne bit her lip and looked unsure. 'Oh, but it's so far away, Robyn, and lonely too!' she said unhappily. 'You'll be so miserable on your own, out in the middle of nowhere.'

'I'll be miserable here!' Robyn replied urgently, grabbing her holdall. 'More than miserable, if I have to face Luke. Please, Anne, this is what I want! Can I have the keys? I need to get away now, before Luke gets here.'

She was away in five minutes. Anne waved her off, watching, nervous and apprehensive, from the upstairs window.

It was a long, long drive from the depths of south-east suburbia, up and across into Wales. You are mad, Robyn told herself, during the five hours of driving, five hours of deliberately concentrating, deliberately forgetting, to go to such lengths, just so you don't have to face him again.

The cottage stood in a field, beneath the shadow of a huge Welsh mountain. It was sparsely furnished, for Anne had only just come into her inheritance, but it was newly decorated and clean.

Robyn dumped her holdall on to the floor and sank on to one of the chintzy sofas. She had made it. Luke wouldn't be able to find her. Anne, true friend that she was, would never give in to him and reveal where the cottage was situated, no matter what bullying tactics he might employ. She was safe.

She closed her eyes and found that she didn't have

the energy to open them again. Sleep was instantaneous and dreamless.

When she awoke, rubbing at a rather stiff neck, feeling hungry, but better than she expected, she found it was the middle of the morning and sunshine was streaming into every corner of the cottage.

The nearest village was about five miles away. Robyn entered the tiny shop and bought at random, grabbing anything that was familiar—an odd assortment of things that would sustain her with the least amount of effort, paying her money to the assistant vaguely, absent-mindedly. There was a telephone box just outside; she had promised to call Anne.

She clutched the change tightly and pressed the combination of numbers. It barely rang. She said quickly, as Anne repeated the number, 'It's me.'

'Oh, Robyn. Are you all right?' Anne asked anxiously. 'We've been so worried about you. Why didn't you phone before?'

'Sorry,' Robyn mumbled, 'I'm sorry. But I'm here. I'm safe.'

There was a moment's silence and then another voice, deep and strong and commanding, came on to the line. 'Robyn, don't hang up! Listen to me. We've got to talk.'

Robyn struggled with herself, wanting to put the phone down, yet needing to hear those urgent, compelling tones just one last time. It was like having a knife twisted in the wound. 'There's nothing to say.' Her voice was thin, strained. 'I don't want to see you again.'

'Robyn! For God's sake! Let me see you, let me explain, talk this through. Where are you? I'll come now. We can sort this out.'

'No,' Robyn ground out, 'Mark's dead. How do you propose to sort that out? He's dead and you helped kill him!'

'You can't honestly believe that!' he murmured in a low, hard voice.

'Why can't I?' Robyn's voice was strident. 'You gave Mark no chance! No support!'

'Robyn, that's not true! He had every chance. Look,

where are you, Robyn?' he demanded patiently. 'Tell me.'

'Don't you understand?' she cried. 'Didn't you hear what I said? I don't want to see you again! I can't!' She could bear no more. Tears streamed down her face; they had done since the first sound of his voice. She slammed down the receiver, struggled against the heavy red door, sobbing uncaringly, and ran past a woman who was waiting to use the phone.

Minutes passed, hours, the rest of that day, and then it was evening again and the prospect of night, long and lonely, haunted her. She couldn't sleep, despite having walked herself into the ground that afternoon, among the sheep and the ferns and the wet grass. She had driven herself on and on, trying to keep her thoughts painless, trying, without success, to think of anything except how badly Luke had hurt her, how easily he had destroyed her life.

By dawn she had cried herself dry. Robyn flung herself around the cottage and searched for paper and pen. She had decided to write to Luke. It was a short note but it took half the morning, a thousand attempts. The cottage was strewn with crumpled, tear-stained paper. She felt she had to do it. Perhaps now, now she had finally written it down, could stare at the irretrievable words, written in black and white, she would be able to accept the way things had to be, she would have the strength to return. It was short, to the point, each sentence more painful than the last.

I owe Mark this. He cared for me, he loved me as I did him. We were flesh and blood. I thought when he died that nothing could ever hurt me so much—now I'm not so sure. I loved you, Luke, somewhere back there, God knows how it happened—or why, because we were always fighting, and when we weren't, in those wonderful, brief moments, I was still constantly aware of what you really thought of me... I am young, naïve perhaps, all the things you said, but I know my own mind, I know what you did to him, what you're doing to me. Leave me alone, Luke. Don't try to see me, because it's pointless. I loved you and I'm ashamed of it. So don't expect me to talk to you. I can't—I won't discuss this. The garden project is over, of course, but, as you've said so many times, there are plenty of other designers. . .

She posted it, felt the emptiness and a deep, deep dullness, more complete than ever before, settle over her. She forced herself to believe she had done the only possible thing.

That day passed so slowly, and the next, the one after that. He would have received it by now, read it. Would it be safe to return, pick up the pieces of her life again? Of course, you fool! she told herself. He's forgotten all about you! About Mark, everything! He's a busy man, with a demanding career. He's important and powerful. Stop kidding yourself. Go back.

The fifth day. She was out walking again. A different route this time around the back of the mountain, over the stream by way of some stepping-stones. Carefully she picked her way across, back to the cottage, for it was getting late. She hadn't eaten in hours. She jumped the last stone, up on to the fern-covered bank.

He was there.

The shock of seeing him, here, now, paralysed her completely. Her heart almost stopped with the pain of having him so near. He had found her! But how? She watched dazedly as he paced in front of the cottage, hands thrust deep into the pockets of his jeans.

He turned suddenly and saw her and she was held motionless by his gaze, caught without any hope of escape, mesmerised by the power and intensity of his whole being. They stood far apart, facing one another across the field, without a word, without a single movement for a long while. Then slowly Luke began to walk towards her, every step bring him closer, increasing Robyn's agony.

'My letter. . .' Her voice was faint.

'Damn your letter!' He came closer, his eyes narrowed in anger. 'I won't accept any of it.'

'Why have you come?' Robyn asked, holding herself rigidly. 'I asked you to leave me alone; I. . .'

'To hell with that!' he snarled. 'Did you honestly expect me to stay home at the barn and carry on as if nothing had happened after you threw all those accusations at me? Murderer and God knows what else! Do you have any idea how long it's taken me to find you in this God-forsaken place? Well?' he demanded savagely, when Robyn didn't reply.

She glared into his face. 'Damn you!' she cried. 'How can you do this to me?' Her voice shook, her face was white with anguish. 'I just can't take it any more. . .can't you see that? Can't you understand that I hate you?' She gave a harsh sob and turned from him, blinded by sudden irrepressible tears.

'Robyn? Oh, God!' he muttered under his breath. 'I promised myself it wouldn't be like this. Darling, I'm sorry, so sorry.' He moved towards and took hold of her gently by the shoulders, forcing her to turn and look at him. 'Robyn, don't turn away from me, please; I didn't mean to be angry. I've driven myself crazy thinking about you, and now I'm here. . . I've been so worried about you.'

She gazed up into his face with bemused wonder and saw an expression there that didn't make sense. She swallowed and took some breaths. 'You called me darling,' she whispered faintly. 'How can you say that?'

He brushed back a strand of copper-coloured hair that had fallen across her face and gazed deep into her eyes. 'With the greatest of ease,' he said softly.

'Don't do this to me,' she whispered unsteadily. 'Don't make it so hard—please, Luke!'

'It's only hard because between us we've made it that way,' he murmured softly. 'These past few days have been a living hell for you and for me.' He gazed down into her emerald eyes. 'Oh, Robyn,' he whispered huskily, 'if only I'd know what you were going through. From the first moment. . .' He put strong, firm hands on to her shoulders, and gazed deep into her eyes. 'I care about you, Robyn. So much. I may not have shown it too well so far. . .'

'But you dislike everything about me,' she breathed. 'You hate the way that I am, the way that I behave. . .'

'Really?' He gave her an intent look, stroked the softness of her cheek. 'Who says?'

'You do!' she replied. 'All the time. . .!' Her voice trailed away unhappily. There was silence.

'I love you.' Luke's voice was deep and magnetic and Robyn felt the anguish twist inside as he gazed into her face, and the once dreamt of words were spoken.

She dragged herself from Luke's grasp and stood a little apart, hugging herself protectively with her arms, as a shield, or as an ineffectual substitute for Luke—she wasn't sure which. 'You can't,' she gasped, eyes wide with wonder and shock.

'I love you,' he repeated, 'more than anything.'

'But Mark. . .don't you understand, it's not possible?' Robyn cried desperately.

'Don't Robyn!' His voice was sharp, the challenge in his ice-blue eyes unmistakable. 'Don't withdraw from me! Mark, his death, how it was in France, it's there, hanging between us. We've got to talk. Until we do talk about it, until you know what went on, we can't move forward. You can't do this, Robyn! I won't let you shut me out!'

'But I don't want to face up to it!' Robyn cried. 'I've spent so long trying to block it all out. It's too painful! Yes,' she said harshly, 'these past days *have* been like a living hell! When I read Mark's letter and found out that it was you. . .' Her voice cracked and she paused, helpless, while her composure fell to pieces around her.

'You can't run away from it forever, Robyn, surely you see that? It's taken you too long to come to terms with Mark's death—Anne told me a little of how it's been with you, the way you've fought the grief and sorrow.' He lowered his voice, came to her and touched the side of her face with one strong hand. 'You can't go on blocking it out. Don't you see? When you received Mark's letter it shocked you, contributed to more pain and agony, but in a way it was a release, a focus for all the anger and misery you've felt at Mark's death. It was such a waste, so avoidable; ever since he died you must have constantly asked yourself why. And then my name.' His voice was grim, his blue eyes intense. 'It was what you needed, wasn't it?'

'No, no, that's not true!' Robyn cried jerkily. 'You don't understand!'

'I understand that you were distraught beyond measure, I understand that Mark's letter came as an almighty shock. What I don't understand,' he added softly, 'is why you didn't give me a chance to tell you how it was from my point of view. Everyone deserves the right of reply.' He gave a rueful smile, which succeeded somehow in melting away the tension. 'Even the arrogant swine Luke Denner needs to put his case from time to time!'

'Luke' she breathed the whisper of his name, gazed up into his face. 'Tell me, then,' she murmured. 'I'll listen.'

'And believe?' he asked gently.

She nodded slowly, meeting his gaze with trusting eyes, praying for this chance, that was her path to happiness. 'And believe,' she repeated.

He took her hand and Robyn felt the strength of him, the warmth seeping through, and then his eyes were grave and he began. 'Robyn, you have to understand that things weren't easy on the film set; time was running out, money was incredibly tight and there were many strong personalities, all, it seemed to me, pulling in opposite directions. Things weren't good—perhaps the film was doomed from the start; I don't know. But from the beginning I sensed that things weren't going to be easy, not for any of us. Mark was nervous, uptight about his role, particularly difficult for him given that this was his first big break in films.' Luke hesitated. 'He was having problems. . .'

'What problems?' Robyn asked quickly.

Luke shook his head. 'He was playing a complicated character; actors with far more experience would have found it difficult—he didn't seem to be able to get a hold of it somehow, to adapt.'

'But you were the director—you could have helped him.'

'Don't you think I tried?' he asked quietly, looking

into her eyes. 'But every time he became so defensive, or aggressive.' He let out a short breath. 'He didn't seem able to accept help.'

Robyn shook her head. 'I don't understand; it's as if you're talking about someone else, some stranger. Mark wasn't like that.'

'Robyn, you've got to understand—Mark was under a lot of pressure; as I've said, this was his first break into the big time, a great deal was expected of him.'

Robyn threw him a puzzled look. 'What are you trying to say?' she demanded quietly. 'Tell me! There's something else, isn't there?'

Luke gazed at her, his eyes blue and penetrating. 'Robyn, Mark had a drink problem.'

'No!'

'Yes!' They had been walking slowly; now he stopped and pulled Robyn around so that she was standing in front of him. 'It's the truth. I wouldn't lie to you about something like this—you know that, surely?'

Robyn crushed her fingers into balls at her side and stared up at him, anguish visible in the emerald of her eyes. 'But he was strong, able, full of life,' she murmured. 'Sure, Mark liked to drink, but he always handled it. Always.'

'Not this time,' Luke replied flatly. 'He used it first, I should imagine, as a way to relax, to loosen up. Soon it became something of a prop.' Luke let out a breath. 'He alternated between aggression and moroseness. We did have an argument that afternoon; he came on to the set clearly hungover—he had been drinking heavily the day before, disrupting things, disturbing the atmosphere. I told him that I wasn't going to tolerate his drinking any longer. He had to get his act together one way or another.' He gave Robyn an intent look. 'I know I'm no angel, Robyn, I know my temper gets the better of me at times, but you must understand the pressure that I was under too. I had to consider so many other things, so many people. Mark had a lot of talent, so much to live for.'

'But surely there was something more you could have done,' Robyn demanded, 'if he needed help?'

'Don't you think I tried?' Luke said gently. 'Earlier, when his drinking first became a problem, I tried to help. I booked him into a clinic, the finest. They could have helped him, but. . .here, read what they had to say.' He delved into his pocket and pulled out several sheets of paper. 'This is the doctor's initial report.'

Robyn took the sheets, holding them shakingly between her fingers, and read enough of the typewritten lines to know that what Luke was saying was the truth. 'What. . .what happened?' she whispered.

Luke's mouth compressed. 'He wouldn't co-operate. Mark discharged himself, came on to the film set and proceeded to tell me what I could do with the part, the film and the crew.'

Poor Mark. It was as Luke said; deep down she knew it, with every part of her soul she knew it. There always had been that part of him, rarely seen, that she didn't understand. Most of the time he had been her Mark: vigorous, full of optimism, never letting anything matter. But sometimes she had seen just a glimpse, a fragment, of an unknown person, deep and inward-looking, complex, full of contradicitons.

Robyn found herself saying, 'So he went for a drive to let off some steam and that was the last. . .'

'Yes,' Luke said grimly.

Robyn swallowed and felt the weakness in her legs. 'And that was how it was?' she murmured flatly.

'My word.'

His word. At one time that would have meant nothing to her; now, she realised, it meant everything.

'Luke. . .' Robyn gazed up into the strong, compelling face. She wanted desperately to reach out and touch the angular cheekbone, to run her fingertips along the firm, sensuous lips. . . 'Thank you,' she whispered unsteadily. 'Thank you for helping Mark; I——'

'Sshh.' Luke lifted his hand and laid it softly against her cheek. 'I did what I could; it's what anyone would have done.'

'No.' Robyn shook her head with certainty. 'No, Luke, not everyone.' She swallowed. 'And. . .and you love me?' Her words were barely audible, so light that they threatened to float away on the breeze.

'With every part of me,' he said, and his voice was rough and a little unsteady and Robyn, in that moment, knew that what he said was true. He stroked a gentle finger along her cheek. 'From the very first moment. But I wouldn't admit it. The charged atmosphere, the tension and electricity whenever we got close—I refused to believe that something so incredible could happen.' He gave a rueful shake of his head, continued stroking her, so that Robyn knew the familiar hypnotism of his touch. 'When you fell in the fountain, when I lifted you out and looked into those fiery green eyes, heard the shaky defiance in your voice, then—then I was lost.'

'But. . .but you were so. . .so. . .'

'Awful? I was a bastard,' he admitted, 'a confused, stubborn son-of-a-bitch!' He gave a rueful shake of his head. 'Luke Denner, you see, didn't know how to handle this girl who fell into his life out of nowhere, who mixed him up and puzzled him too, because there was something, someone else beneath the surface. Love at first sight. Not a condition that mature, worldly Luke Denner ever believed in, and I fought it every step of the way.'

'You were mean,' Robyn murmured.

'Yes.'

'And angry.'

'That, too. But not all of the time. When you awoke, crying from that dream, all my resolve melted. To comfort you, to hold you and make everything all right—that was all that mattered.'

'But you thought I was pregnant. . .' Robyn's voice trailed away unhappily, as she remembered how it had felt to have him reject her.

'Melissa put the idea of pregnancy into my head,' he murmured grimly. 'I see now what a mistake it was to listen to her, but she planted the seed quite naturally, in her own devious little way, and I thought about it, torturing myself with the knowledge that it was a possibility. I asked you that night because I couldn't go on not knowing one way or the other. When you left me. . .well,' he added after a pause, 'let's say I wasn't too thrilled. Now I know that when I had made love to you that afternoon I was right to follow my instincts.'

'Why didn't you tell me how you felt?' Robyn whispered.

'Because you were so vulnerable, I felt it had been unfair of me to take advantage of you.'

'And you cared about that?' Robyn asked wonderingly.

'More than anything,' he replied. 'I didn't want anything to hurt you. . .' He paused and gave her an intense look that revealed a little of how it had been for him. 'I've been fighting the inevitable for too long, darling. It wasn't until the party that I knew I couldn't pretend to myself any longer. And then something happened,' he continued. 'I felt you were lost to me and I couldn't understand why.'

'Mark's letter.' Robyn's voice shook, but she forced the words out. 'I read it and felt as if my world was gone. Loving you, it was all I wanted, and then when I read his words. . . I'm sorry, Luke. But I was so distraught, so hurt. . . I made such a mess of things. . .'

Robyn gazed up at the billowing white clouds and a longing for Luke's touch, unlike anything she had ever felt before, overwhelmed her completely—her whole being ached with the desire to be held in his arms, to feel the strength and comfort and warmth of his body close to hers. She needed him so badly, yet he made no move towards her. I love you! she yelled silently, staring up at the skies. Can't you see how I feel? Can't you sense it?

The clouds were scudding across the expanse of blue; Robyn watched them, mesmerised by their constantly changing shapes. Then strangely the sun began to turn black and the sky dark and as she breathed the shadow of his name she felt her legs folding beneath her and in a moment she had fainted.

When she came to, she saw that he was carrying her across the field, past the cottage and up the track towards his Jaguar. She felt deep relief and sank back into his arms, allowing exhaustion to overtake her. 'Where are we going?' she whispered.

He gazed down at her then and she felt the brief, searing taste of his mouth on hers. 'Home,' he replied huskily.

The word sounded good—warm and familiar. 'To the barn?'

He placed her gently on her feet and opened the car door, keeping his arms close around her all the while. 'Where else?' he murmured. 'The scene of so many mistakes. I've fought how I feel about you for so long; now I want to take you there, to put every one of them right.' He lowered his head then and she saw the deep, intense passion in his eyes, felt the searing heat race through her body. And then his mouth fell to hers and he consumed her with hungry possession.

She slept the whole journey, content in the knowledge that Luke was beside her, in control, in her heart.

When they arrived at the barn, he led her silently by the hand, through the living-room, and then up along the gallery to his bedroom. He paused outside the door.

'I love you, Robyn,' he murmured. 'And I want to show you how much again.' His mouth brushed her lips and Robyn felt the strength of his arms as he scooped her up and carried her through the doorway.

Slowly, slowly he undressed her, kissing each patch of pale, smooth skin, as it was revealed to him, stroking her, touching her all the while, until she lay before him on the huge expanse of bed, in the lacy fragments of her underwear—the only barrier between Luke and her nakedness. She saw the way his eyes roamed her body, lingering on the full curves of her breasts, the flat plane of her stomach, and then he removed his shirt, his jeans, so that once again she knew the thrill of seeing his gleaming, naked torso. Her eyes fell irresistibly to the firm, broad chest, the gleam of hard, taut muscle and then he was pulling her to him, kissing her mouth, her neck, the base of her throat, finding the clasp of her bra, discarding it, so that her breasts hung heavy and exposed, aching with longing and desire.

Robyn watched as his hands moulded and caressed each silken mound, heard the gasp of delight escape from her own lips as his fingers played with the darkened peaks.

She touched him, her hands flat against his chest, tangling in the dark, dark hair, following its trail that led down and down, stroking the aroused maleness that would be a part of her so very, very soon.

The sheets were cool beneath her heated, voluptuous body. He was above her, strong and sure and powerful, wanting her, needing her, loving her. He kissed her lips, then trailed his mouth with tantalising slowness down over her breasts, her stomach, her thighs, lingering at the place where passion focused itself. Robyn gasped incoherently as his mouth played and teased, felt the moistness of desire increasing until she wondered dazedly whether she could endure such ecstasy any longer.

'My darling Robyn, you're so lovely, so pure, so sweet. I've loved you from the very first moment I saw you. So many times I've wanted to do this again. . .so many times. . .' His words scorched her skin. She felt the command of his hands as they moved apart her pliant thighs, the move of his body so that now he was almost there, almost hers.

'Please, Luke!' she gasped as he moved against her. 'I love you, I love you! Make me yours!'

'I want you now, now and forever,' he murmured huskily. 'Marry me, darling, say you'll be my wife,'

Ecstasy increased as Robyn looked deep into his eyes and heard the words she had hardly dared hoped for. 'Yes, Luke,' she cried. 'Oh, yes!'

And then he entered her and she felt the sudden glorious thrust of possession as together they reached the pinnacle of pleasure and he took her heart and soul forever—with his love.

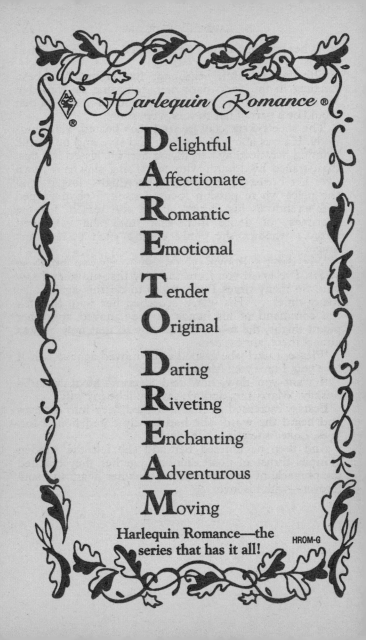

Harlequin Romance ®

Delightful
Affectionate
Romantic
Emotional

Tender
Original

Daring
Riveting
Enchanting
Adventurous
Moving

Harlequin Romance—the
series that has it all!

HROM-G

HARLEQUIN PRESENTS®

HARLEQUIN PRESENTS
men you won't be able to resist falling in love with...

HARLEQUIN PRESENTS
women who have feelings just like your own...

HARLEQUIN PRESENTS
powerful passion in exotic international settings...

HARLEQUIN PRESENTS
intense, dramatic stories that will keep you turning
to the very last page...

HARLEQUIN PRESENTS
The world's bestselling romance series!

◈ Harlequin®
Historical

If you're a serious fan of historical romance,
then you're in luck!

Harlequin Historicals brings you
stories by bestselling authors, rising new stars
and talented first-timers.

Ruth Langan & Theresa Michaels
Mary McBride & Cheryl St.John
Margaret Moore & Merline Lovelace
Julie Tetel & Nina Beaumont
Susan Amarillas & Ana Seymour
Deborah Simmons & Linda Castle
Cassandra Austin & Emily French
Miranda Jarrett & Suzanne Barclay
DeLoras Scott & Laurie Grant...

You'll never run out of favorites.

Harlequin Historicals...they're too good to miss!

HH-GEN

HARLEQUIN®

INTRIGUE®

THAT'S INTRIGUE—DYNAMIC ROMANCE AT ITS BEST!

Harlequin Intrigue is now bringing you more—more men and mystery, more desire and danger. If you've been looking for thrilling tales of contemporary passion and sensuous love stories with taut, edge-of-the-seat suspense—then you'll *love* Harlequin Intrigue!

Every month, you'll meet four new heroes who are guaranteed to make your spine tingle and your pulse pound. With them you'll enter into the exciting world of Harlequin Intrigue—where your life is on the line and so is your heart!

Harlequin Intrigue—we'll leave you breathless!

INT-GEN

LOOK FOR OUR FOUR FABULOUS MEN!

Each month some of today's bestselling authors bring
four new fabulous men to Harlequin American Romance.
Whether they're rebel ranchers, millionaire power brokers
or sexy single dads, they're all gallant princes—and
they're all ready to sweep you into lighthearted fantasies
and contemporary fairy tales where anything is possible
and where all your dreams come true!

You don't even have to make a wish...Harlequin American
Romance will grant your every desire!

Look for Harlequin American Romance wherever Harlequin
books are sold!